ISBN 978-1-68487-644-0

This book has been published with all efforts taken to make the material error-free after the consent of the author. However, the author and the publisher do not assume and hereby disclaim any liability to any party for any loss, damage, or disruption caused by errors or omissions, whether such errors or omissions result from negligence, accident, or any other cause. While every effort has been made to avoid any mistake or omission, this publication is being sold on the condition and understanding that neither the author nor the publishers or printers would be liable in any manner to any person by reason of any mistake or omission in this publication or for any action taken or omitted to be taken or advice rendered or accepted on the basis of this work. For any defect

My dear

Supportive Figure Of My Life - My CHULLU - dear Wife , My Parents and Kapil(who support me in writing this book)

I wrote this story for you, but when I began it I had not realized that time passes quicker than books. I shall probably be happy for your honest review, for which your are famous of & wish to listen a word from you say about

this book

Your Affectionate Dear

ADESH KUMAR SINGH

Index

" I wrote my story in such a way that even people who understand it still end up crying "

FOUR STEPS TOWARDS HELL

The story begins in 2003 when we were supposed to be 15 years old according to the rules, but based on our documents, we were actually just 13 years old. Nowadays, we also see our own children through the lens of childhood, sometimes our parents also forget to see us from these perspectives. It was April 17 that day, on which exactly God cut off our umbilical cord from our birthplace and sent us to our college hostel.

When the family came to drop us at the hostel, many thoughts crossed their minds - how will our child live so far away from home, manage without home-cooked meals, and stay away from home.

Lost in this worry, when they handed over our belongings in the hostel room, near the main gate of the school, they were worried about how we would stay so far away from them., Somewhere, right? But what did they know at the time of farewell, that despite standing at their gate, we would not even look back towards the hostel even once.

We were like free birds who had just been released from the family constraints and suddenly found all the joy of life. We were not the ones sent here because we wanted to, but because one of our neighbors, another goat of our age, was sent with us to be slaughtered together.

The name of this new roommate was - Sameer.

But we were pleasantly surprised to find out that Sameer was even more miserable than us without his family. After bidding farewell to our families, we returned to our hostel room. However, as soon as we entered the room, it felt like our senses were blown away, because the environment was completely different from when we had entered with our families. we thought, were all the innocent children, the good ones living in this room?

Because now the room was in a different condition and not just ours, all the rooms had a similar condition. Oh, I made a mistake - I forgot to tell you a brief description of the hostel and our college. Our college was located in a village named Govardhan near Mathura district in Uttar Pradesh, secluded from the hustle and bustle of the market.

A little further away, it was all just village after village. You all must know that since ancient times, we all have preferred such places and colleges for hostels. Due to this preference, we were also brought here.

In this college known for its good English medium education as well as cultural heritage, there were two separate hostels - one for boys and the other, as you may have guessed - a concentration center (a place where by concentrating, our entire boys' hostel used to increase its concentration power, and also another for girls).

Let's get straight to the point, the second thing was, your and our own Galser hostel. Just like we think about the Galser Hostel, maybe there's also a talk about the Boys Hostel there. These two accommodation centers (Boys and girls hostel) were located right in front of each other within the school campus.

Ask for some demand to stick if there's no road between both buildings then they will just stick to each other. (Oh, I'm talking about sticking the buildings together, nothing else, what you were thinking is also true)

The hostel building was 5 storeys high, with 8 big rooms on each floor and 15 to 20 kids in each room, with good arrangements for beds and wardrobes.

The entire hostel was the responsibility of a Hostel Warden appointed by the school, who lived on the bottom floor of the hostel and made efforts to control the entire hostel from there.

Our room was on the fifth floor of the hostel, separate and famous by the name of Room number 17. Information about our room being famous in the hostel reached us within a few hours, and the reasons for it too.

WELCOME TO HELL

In the Sanskar School, when our family members left, when we both friends returned after their departure, the room was in a bit of a mess. The classmate Rohan, who had put a mark on our parents' feet, was now praising the teacher with helping verbs of mothers and sisters. To avoid the teacher's praise from falling short, some more helping verbs were used besides mother and sisters.

In the class, Kuldeep was taking a shower and praying - in front of our father and now in front of our parents, he was rinsing his mouth with a betel nut in his mouth, directing a 1st class child in the room to get water with his mother.

There were a total of 16 children in our room, out of which 4 were seniors of our larger classes, two were us - in class 9th, and the rest of the children were from smaller classes ranging from 6 to 8 years.

Not only that, as soon as our eyes fell on the most senior brother in the room, Purushottam, my and Sameer's hair stood on end. Purushottam had a slipper in his hand and had all the young children sitting in front of him. And while pulling the children's hair, he was asking, "What! One of you needed to wash your underwear today?" As soon as Purushottam found out whose underwear it was, he called the child to him and started beating him with slippers and said, "Tonight, your punishment is to sleep."

Seeing all this, my and Sameer's hair stood on end, as it was the same Purushottam who, in front of our parents, was pointing out his physics, with his ears closed, sitting on his bed reading, and telling my parents, "Uncle, if I have a test tomorrow, can you go out and talk?" Our biggest worry was that when Purushottam was saying this, our other seniors Kuldeep, Rohan, and Mayank were all laughing out loud.

Samir asked me, "Dude, I didn't understand the deal of the sleeping punishment, does it mean that everyone stays awake at night here and only one sleeps?" Upon hearing Samir's words, I was completely in suspense, and only one thought was running through both of our minds, 'Where did we get stuck, buddy?' But looking at Mayank, we were somewhat satisfied thinking maybe there is a senior here who will side with us. We had just assumed that Mayank would welcome us into the room with 15-20 helping verbs. Thank God, he was the first one to do so.

Hearing the child crying from Purushottam's hit, Samir called him over to sit with us. Even before they came into our room, they had two reasons - one to calm down Purushottam, and the other to offer us both a warm welcome. Finally, it was the first day for both of us in the school and hostel.

Mayank was sitting with the rest of the seniors when Samir was called over. I was standing there thinking maybe someone would be scolded or maybe someone would be sent to fill a bottle, but when I heard the words coming out of the senior's mouth in front of me, my head was spinning. The senior opened the window and pointed towards the hostel, saying to Samir, "Look, you are new in the hostel today, so whatever you do, it will seem like a mistake.

And if our name is associated with being caught in anything, then there will be a beating for you there on the same day and here in the room every day. Maybe Pramod has shown you around already." Samir, trembling, said, "B...b...b...brother, so, so what should I do, please make it a bit easier." Mayank said, "Haha, don't worry, we will make it very easy for you.

You just have to go to that roof in front and see that girl who is drying clothes on the roof. Once she leaves, grab the two smallest pieces of clothes from all those clothes." Samir said, "B...bro...brother, I don't... I don't understand. Smallest means." Mayank quieted Samir down and said to Purushottam to his friend, "Hey Kushagra you are the smallest boy of the 10th class, give your contribution in serving the new kids too."

This was the first time I had seen Kushagra; his hair was slightly big, his eyes were confused. At Purushottam's insistence, Kushagra came up to Samir and started asking, "Which is the smallest piece of clothing on your body?" I took out my handkerchief from my pocket and signaled towards Samir, indicating him to tell it, but when Samir gestured towards his T-shirt, Kushagra quickly pulled his lower down and grabbed Samir's underwear, saying, "Hey idiot, you have to bring this.

From the roof in front." Hearing this, Samir put on his lower and gestured towards me with his eyes, as if asking me what to do, and then I also lowered my eyes and shook my hands in a way as if there was no other option left. Samir left the room to complete his mission. I was still thinking about the discussion going on in the room between

In front, on the roof of the hostel, Mayank had seen that girl with clothes on, the rest of the guys weren't in the room. Kushagra asked Mayank about that girl, who was sent for him. Mayank said, "Oh, that was 'Saj'." After hearing this, all the guys started cursing Mayank and scolded him. Kushagra also angrily said to Mayank, "You scoundrel, you sent him to get clothes from Saj Khan, she is your sister-in-law, she is going to be our begum." Meanwhile, Purushottam slapped a little boy's ear and sent him to call Samir back quickly.

All the guys were talking to each other and were worried. Kuldeep said, "Oh God, someone catch a teacher and stop Samir, just in case he sees Saj bringing clothes." Mayank said, "Saj was pulling this crazy girl from the fourth floor by holding onto her leg, just like she did with that guy two months ago."

After hearing all this, one thing stuck in my mind that Samir went to work today. I was scared about Samir because as he was running into the room, he took out his clothes from his pocket and gave them to the guys, saying, "Here you go, bro, your work is done."

Everyone started praising Samir and telling him how brave he was today. Kushagra, for some reason, seemed worried among all of them, while everyone else was happy and saying, "The boy has come back from the mouth of death." Just then, cutting off his words, pointing angrily at me, he called me in a rage, asked for my name, and started saying to me, "Look dude, your friend has done a very brave thing and now we need to check how much bravery you have, so we need to check this cloth and bring it back to where Samir brought it from." After that, Kushagra came forward and said to me, "Hey, listen, put your hand on the door and check where the door comes from, and bring it back from there." This was the first moment in my life when I understood the true use of a proverb. When I was asked to go to Girls Hostel holding that cloth, I was on cloud nine. I hesitated and started saying in my home language - "I won't go there at Balko mere Lal, make me do something else."

Pointing to Kushagra, he said, "I can do a job for you. I will convince your Saj." All the guys burst out laughing and Kushagra said, "Come on, brothers, let's help him." Then he said to me, "You will convince Saj from tomorrow.

." Forget golf, if you messed up even the dishwashing, you'll be my disciple. And until you manage to do that, you have no other way. It was fixed in my mind that I had to take Samir and run away from here in the night. Hostel was not important, nor was the studying. They all were looking at me so I understood that they were testing me for my answer. Showing confidence in my words, I said to the teacher - "I will soon become your guru." After hearing all this, Purushottam said - "Listen, show that item to this kid tomorrow. Son, he's a fighter plane."

The meeting ended and the day faded away. On the first day, when Samir and I returned to the room after having dinner with everyone at 8:00 PM, two teachers were already seated in the room, whom all the kids were addressing as PTI Sir with respect.

I understood even before entering the room that something was wrong. When everyone seemed worried during dinner, upon entering the room, I saw both teachers holding a cricket stump in each hand, one had a stick against Kuldeep's neck. Going further, the matter was explained by the Sir that in the evening, at the time of lights out, he was jumping from the school boundary. Just then, at the right moment, Kuldeep was caught.

For the next 20 minutes in the room, both PTI Sirs attended to Kuldeep excellently, and just when the service was about to end, an idea struck one PTI to check Kuldeep's cupboard. After checking the cupboard, when they found some betel nut spices outside, Kuldeep revealed where all those betel nut spices came from, there was a new entry in the diary of your hostel's Shogar.

By repeatedly showing his teeth to the PTI sir, Shogar wasn't wrong, but within the PTI's pocket check, two cigarettes played a significant role in souring the basket. After 45 minutes, when the service story ended, with both pundits giving advice and leaving, Kuldeep and Shogar were still in a continuing assistance but other students in the remaining room burst into laughter. They made fun of the two of them, leaving us out of it. Since we were still caught in the same dilemma - whether to run away from here or not. Thankful that maybe some divine power had made everything clear to me,

Thanks to any lord that i got on time the real sense.

But it seems like our brother Sameer had a shadow of Rahu over his mind. He made up his mind that he wouldn't stop here for even a moment, and when he didn't agree to run away home with me, he left, feeling so sorry for me that for the next 2 hours, he didn't talk to anyone about him.

Just to reach the bus stop, he even picked up someone's cycle from the hostel. I also got to know about the cycle incident a little late. The night passed with changing positions. But on the second day, we were both in full form, finally our first day at school. Wearing new uniforms and new shoes, we were also feeling no less than any Shahrukh Khan. Feeling proud, we hung our school bag on one shoulder, humming a song as we walked towards the school gate.

One thing was clear in our minds, that bowing down in front of anyone here meant your downfall. So keeping this in mind, we went to the last seat in class and put our bags down with style.

It was for sure that even in the future our luck wasn't going to be good because just a little while later we were going to face a dangerous predator, but there was still some time left for that.

We patted our bag on the seat and stepped out of the school to feel the outside air. As we looked at the air and the other classes, we remembered one thing about the hostel kids that the school's toilets are more beautiful than the school's classes. So, without any delay, we stepped towards the toilet. When we reached the toilet, we saw that it was actually quite nice, it looked as if it was some VIP place.

But just a few moments later, our hair was standing on end, our eyes were wide, and our body was all goosebumps because we saw a big girl naked for the first time in our lives, we couldn't take our eyes off her for a few moments, but as soon as she got up, we felt like she might turn around and see us, so we turned back and went back.

But by then, it was already too late because in just a few seconds when we came out of the washroom, that girl was standing in front of us, first she whispered something in English in our ears with a high voice, in which some Hindi abuses were also included.

Just a while as if we didn't even realize what was happening in front of us because we knew the mistake was ours, so we convinced ourselves quietly that son, keep listening quietly, but she was not ready to stay quiet.

And when she showed us in a little while that now a strong slap was coming towards our cheek, we remembered our own words - "Son, bend down or you'll get chopped." So, what was left, we also bent down and said to her – "Listen, whatever you want to say to me, say it now. It's my first day, so I made a mistake accidentally, and that's why I haven't said anything till now - don't come in front of me next time."

After hearing this, she grunted with irritation and said - "I will come like this every day in front of you and I will also give you the same treatment every day, understand that you meet people like you every day who should be chopped. Saying this, I repeated my words, that go, meet people like you every day who should be chopped. With these words, I walked towards the class and she was screaming from behind - "You will only bear one heavy blow in your life, it's a big deal for you to endure for the second one." I went to the class and lay down on the bag with my face down.

In just 15 minutes, my morning was peacefully calm when a class 10th student shouted from outside and called me. I was in 9th grade and the student calling me was from the parallel class of ours, in the 10th grade. When I reached the student, he took me to his class.

The prayer was about to start in another 10 minutes, so both of us went and sat on a seat in class 10th. The student then showed me his crush and said, "Look brother, she is the same girl for whom my brothers have a crush petition." I was once again in a dilemma, she was the same girl whose image was now etched in my mind, and again, she came with a rose in her hand towards me. She was continuously staring at me and for the sake of appearances, I too was looking at her, while the student was constantly glancing at both of us to see what would happen in the end. Thankfully, the prayer bell rang, and I found an excuse to leave from there.

I did go to the prayer, but in my mind, only the face of that girl kept running. Whatever you say, the girl had charm. She was the first girl I had seen who made all the guys like a Purushottam scared. Even though both of us were seemingly hating each other, somewhere her attitude and the air of disliking boys appealed to me.

Standing at 5 feet 3 inches tall, she had a slight round face, a little long, fair facial skin, straight hair falling to one side of her forehead, eyes that seemed to be tinged with a greenish hue against black color, and she had applied strawberry flavor to her lips a day earlier. She wasn't wrong at all, although everyone might call her pretty but for me, she was something different.

She was an enemy for me, and some of her habits I also fancied. Every time I thought of her, the same words would come to my mind - Rose Khan - and after that my heart had given her a name - ROSE KHAN. Maybe her charm had turned every 'routine' day into 'Rose' days in my mind. These thoughts were running through my mind in prayer.

As soon as she looked at me with a stare upon entering the class, I also made a dirty gesture with my hand and then she angrily went to her class, and I went angrily to mine.

This was our first class in school. It started with the introduction of the students. Everyone was being asked what they want to become in life, some were saying doctor, some engineer, some teacher. The reason for wanting to become all this was also being asked from all the children. Everyone was sharing their choices. Before my turn came, I was also getting anxious thinking what to become. I thought let's see what happens, but the question was what do I tell this teacher because he was asking cross-questions to everyone. Finally, sitting on the last seat, we were the last to go.

Just before our number was called, when we couldn't think of anything new to say, after giving our introduction, we mistakenly said to the teacher - "Sir, we will ask our senior classmates and tell you later what we want to become." That strict teacher seemed like he didn't know what to say, he asked a child from the front seat to call the 10th class first position holder because he will tell them what they want to become in life.

That child went to call, but after hearing the teacher, the entire class burst into laughter. That's when I realized that in the quest to do well, I had embarrassed myself in class. As luck would have it, the 10th class topper completed it because the topper sir had called me in the class to decide my future, she was Saj Khan, also known as 'Rose Khan' (Roj - Roj every day).

The teacher called Rose to the front of the class and then called me too. When I reached in front with her, the teacher said to me, "Here comes the topper, finalize your future."

There was only one thought in my mind. I couldn't figure out whether I should blame this teacher or this girl first. In the midst of all this, I fell silent and wondered why I was called. I was just thinking, "Oh God! Have you filled this in my destiny or is it a little too peaceful, I put my hand on my mouth as an excuse to vomit and left the class. I came back to the class after 10 minutes and found Rose sitting in the same class.

Seeing her there, only I could understand what I went through. In my class, the teacher singled him out in front of me. I had understood the teacher's plan; his whole intention was to end my embarrassing moment period.

As I was leaving my seat, I said, "Sir, I want to be a killer because their demand is everywhere, in big leaders, in big people, and the biggest benefit of becoming a killer is that if someone starts to act smart in front of you or is too arrogant, just put them in their place right there." Daily while saying this, she turned to the teacher and said, "Sir, let's go to the class, if this is over."

Then she went back to her class. The day passed somehow and in the evening, all the hostel children went to the field to play sports. After the sports time was over in our hostel, all the children would have an evening prayer. I was shocked to see Samir standing in front of his father. I understood that Uncle Auntie had come to take him back, but both PT teachers were taking out chocolates from their pockets and giving them to Samir, so all the children were laughing during the evening prayer, and I was silently saying to myself that "Hey, both of you, don't eat it all, keep one for me," and by that time, Samir had already eaten another chocolate.

I don't know why my eyes would always meet his every day. Meanwhile, PT teachers were lovingly explaining to Samir, "Bad habits, don't go back to such hostels." On the other hand, my eyes would meet hers every day, and Shahnaaz, who looked just like her, was standing behind her.

At the time when Shahnaaz, who would stare at me daily, sent me a flying kiss with a smile, my head was spinning. Kushagra commented from behind, "Hey, this guy will get beaten up, stay away from them in fights." In a short while, a teacher passed by me and whispered in my ear pointing towards Shahnaaz, "Son, one teacher was trapped by these two sisters, well, will you serve soon or not."

I immediately turned towards the front and saw something else in front of me. Uncle Auntie had left Samir and gone. Samir's face was covered with chocolate, and both his hands were held by different teachers. And the PT teacher was ready behind Samir with a stick ready to start beating. With the fast-paced and anxious voices, Samir's service was started.

The PTI sir was beating from behind, while the other PTI sir was giving a strong fielding on Samir's chocolate-filled cheeks with his hands. Whatever you say, I shouldn't have been happy seeing this sight, but my chest was filled with happiness.

I felt extremely proud of the hostel fellows who didn't run away. In the feeling of this pride, hearing Samir's loud whistles felt like all the tiredness of the day had disappeared. The show ended and all the kids headed towards the hostel saying the name of God. Samir was walking with me.

I praised him that he really tackled a great hit. Then I asked Samir if he was enjoying watching the hits as much as he was enjoying eating. I chuckled, and Samir, looking at me angrily, walked into the room. With two days' experience in the hostel, two things became clear to me - first, if you bow down, you will get cut - second, the hostel is a place where animal language is spoken. Indeed, the experience in front of me completed it. At night, when Samir and I were sleeping, I suddenly heard a child crying in his sleep.

When I got up and turned on the light, I saw a small child of 6 to 7 years old with Purushottam covered in a blanket. Seeing Purushottam's dirty behavior, my hair stood on end, because he continued his bad behavior even after seeing me. I tried to tell all this about Purushottam to Kuldip and Rohan, and saw that they too were indulging in the same misbehavior with the other kids on their respective beds. Seeing all this, I was completely shocked and turned off the light and went out of the room.

After mustering up the courage, I was just about to go to the warden to tell him all this when I saw him going towards the room of the maid who takes care of the little kids. Before I reached the gate of the room, the door was closed from the inside.

I was completely speechless. Back in my room, struggling to muster the courage to tell him all this.

I didn't have the courage to see all of that. Whatever I had seen were all thoughts coming in front of my eyes. And I, confused, sat in the hostel. I couldn't understand anything and what should I do.

When I understood, one thing came to mind that there is Don't be bow down here at any cost.....

"Street smart knowledge"

One thing was for sure, if you wanted to make it big in this jungle, you had to be a big animal. But I had also thought that everything has to be done in such a way that no teacher or school management could even point a finger at me. I knew that my family had sent me here for a reason. And when I had to become a big shot, I also knew that being big means being the biggest in everything. I had to be the worst of the worst and the best of the best. For all this, I had made a plan for myself that after the class ended, I didn't want to go to the hostel like all the other kids.

After the class ended, I would finish all my writing work, and then I would sit in the same class, revising everything that was taught by the teacher that day. After school hours, for one and a half hours, I fixed everything for my parents' sake. And after one and a half hour, I was going to be king of the Hell.

I told you all this because I thought I could make you understand that you can do anything in life. Don't let anything come between your hopes and dreams, and never let anyone stop you. Days kept passing by. As the days went by, our arguments also kept increasing multiple times.

Because of arguments, many times, we had to go to the principal's office, manager's office, and even the director's office. Many times, when we faced each other, we used to end up arguing about something. From the girl's side, Shahnaaz, and from the boy's side, Kushagra, both used to manage this dispute when necessary. Along with hostel life, school life was also full of adventures. Such as falling asleep quietly in class, feeling happy when a friend got scolded by the teacher, exchanging chemicals in the chemistry lab.

All these moments were part of our memories, although some bad incidents also happened. For example, due to a prank involving wrong experiments with chemicals in the chemistry lab, two of my friends got their hands burned, and one even got his face burned. That made us realize not to repeat all these mistakes.

Oh! We forgot about a dangerous subject, your and our biology. As you all know, because of a few chapters in the biology subject, things get a different turn in the mind. And if we didn't lie, our minds were also working in a very twisted way. Like all of you, we also wanted to grasp the knowledge of those 2-3 chapters together. But the level of our misunderstanding was different as we had more expectations from the biology lab just like our chemistry and physics labs.

To be honest, we were eagerly waiting for the day when this chapter arrived and boys and girls were taken together to the biology lab. Our heart was just yearning for that day. But our wishful happiness couldn't last long as along with Purushottam, other seniors shattered our happiness by revealing the true nature of the biology lab.

We were lost in this shock for 2-3 days, wondering if in reality in the biology lab, we just observed some specimens and slides under the microscope. And the only thought that came to our minds was asking our seniors in a group, "Sister thief, where will we get the knowledge of this chapter from now?"

All the answers were different, but as usual, we liked Saurabh's solution. According to Saurabh, the Boys' Hostel was just one floor away from the Girls' Hostel, Saurabh's 10th C "mystery" meter. All the kids used to address Saurabh as "meter."

Everyone in the hostel knew that Saurabh was the biggest, quiet, and aloof one. Some kids used to attribute his aloofness to a girl from the Girls' Hostel, Vandana. That's why the kids had given him the nickname Devdas. According to Saurabh, if both of us (me and Saurabh) manage to reunite

Saurabh with Vandana, then Vandana will easily give us full knowledge of this chapter.

So, what we did was, we created a roadmap with three steps in our minds - the first step, sneaking into Saurabh's heart - the second step, the reunion of Saurabh and Vandana, and the third, where both of us joyfully visualized in our minds - Vandana will give us complete knowledge of the chapter together. That's how the workaround was achieved.

KNOWLEDGE OF THE BIOLOGY CHAPTER

It was night time and me and Kushagra were both sitting on the hostel rooftop. The reason we were sitting on the rooftop was Saurav shuffler. It was 1:00 am. Saurabh shuffler was sitting in a corner humming a song and constantly teasing the girls hostel. Most of the kids in the hostel were scared of Saurabh shuffler, because whenever a kid disturbed him, he used to retaliate quite directly in return. Kushagra and I knew Saurabh's weakness. That's why we had already ordered a bottle of wine for the kids coming daily from home.

The problem was also that neither me nor Kushagra drank wine. We both wanted to keep this whole matter to ourselves because we were afraid that if the kids increased, they might stop giving us respect in Vandana Bio chapter. We were on one corner of the rooftop and Saurav shuffler was on the room facing the girls hostel.

We both had a long argument about who should go to Saurav shuffler first. In the end, Kushagra took the glass and bottle and went to shuffler. Kushagra offered the bottle to him, but shuffler couldn't refuse. I also reached him while roaming. As per shuffler's request, I lied and said that Kushagra had ordered the bottle for himself. If I didn't say so, shuffler would have doubted that we were conspiring against him.

After that, Kushagra had to drink with shuffler, which was beyond our planning. Before asking shuffler about Vandana, Kushagra started shouting towards the windows of the girls hostel- "Hey folks! Come out" and "Come out, let's go outside" and began creating a scene. It seemed like he was saying that to some cat wandering on the road in his state of intoxication.

But as soon as the girls hostel window opened, I saw daily squinting at the door on the other side and I panicked and stepped back. I didn't see his face again but I heard him say from his ears -

"Wait, I'm coming upstairs." Both of them were sitting on the balcony of the girls hostel. I was just wondering what to do next? Then suddenly I saw two or three girls coming towards the front rooftop. I immediately lay down on the side of the balcony as if they didn't see me.

But when there are friends, there is no need for enemies. There were two girls with daily. Who were standing in front of Kushagra and Saurav shuffler on the opposite rooftop. I quickly understood that the guy must have drunk for the first time today, the drama has to be solid. But I didn't expect what was about to happen.

Ku Kushagra had a unique way of dealing with friendships and enmities. In a playful manner, he would say, "Hey buddy, why are you lying down here scared? Get up!" Without understanding anything, I replied, "No buddy, I was just picking up some snacks from below, why would I be scared of this?"

I remembered Shahnaaz's flying kick incident and some small jokes as well. I picked up the wine bottle and gestured towards Shahnaaz. She started giggling, and I was pondering why the teacher and other kids discouraged her confidence. Amidst all this, I unintentionally got into a daily argument without thinking.

In this argument, I kept saying every day, "Because of you, Saurabh is like this. If you didn't provoke Vandana, everything would be fine between them." I was trying hard to make Kushagra say something because every word of his meant a possible murder the next day. That's why I was getting into a daily argument without even thinking. And in these arguments, I kept saying every day, "Because of you, Saurabh is like this.

If you didn't provoke Vandana, everything would be fine between them." Juhi gave some clarification about it, and the watchman shouted from below. They went to the hostel room, and we went to ours. We thought the story would end there, but how could the fight between us end? The next day, we were studying in class when we were called to the principal's office. In the office, I, Kushagra , and Saurav were told the same thing, "You guys have become goons, getting drunk at night and harassing girls." Everyone else was saved from this allegation, but I couldn't bear the accusation of harassing girls. And I burst out saying, "All of this is a complete lie. Otherwise, call which girl is saying this." It was the first time he was sent for calling from the office.

And I was standing in full mood thinking that as soon as he comes in daily, I have to call his office. I was just waiting for him when I heard someone coming from behind. I heard the steps of Kamini and Shahnaaz giggling as she entered the office. And she started questioning me while still smiling, "Did you not pick up the liquor bottle and gesture towards me for a drink? You..."

She was still smiling as she asked this, and I was remembering the teacher who had taken me aside for an explanation during the evening prayer, but I couldn't remember...

And about all those kids who used to tell me about it. Shahnaaz didn't seem enough. Then she said, "Sir, they won't listen like this. This is their daily job. You should write a complaint against them so that next time this happens, their names can be taken."

I was still staring at this girl with eyes wide open, trying to figure out if she was really the same girl who gave me the flying kiss. And who used to tease me. And most importantly, the elephant whisperer actually took her words as if it was an order from the gods. Finally, after leaving us a warning note, she also left. Shahnaaz came out of the office with us. While heading out of the office, I was still in shock as I kept looking towards her, she came up to me and started asking, "Were you just thinking about the flying kiss scene inside the office?

And all that stuff that I was talking to you about?" In response to this question, I didn't say anything, and she continued, "I know you felt uncomfortable, but I did all of that for you. I want to see you become a better person." I was looking at her angrily, and all of a sudden, Kusum interrupted, "Yes, Shahnaaz is very nice, but look, this crazy one never agreed with us." Kusum added, "Now you agree that Shahnaaz is so nice." And I just said, "Even a hundred times better." While talking like this, we all went back to our respective classes. I sat in class for 5 minutes

When Rose called me out and asked me to leave the class. The teacher asked me to step outside, and when I got there, she said, "Listen, you know what you said yesterday - I asked 'What'?" I said, "We were discussing Vandana and Saurav. You were right, that's why we asked Vandana to do whatever she wants.

I hope she and Saurav become one from today." This was the first time in life when we were talking so lovingly to each other.

I kept moving the conversation forward and said daily, "By the way, Rose, you also ..." I had just said this when she interrupted me and said, "Okay, now don't go overboard, just listen to what I told you. As for you or boys, I keep boys here on their toes."

After saying this, she left, and while scolding myself internally, I was still trying to convince myself to break my own rule. My same rule - 'If you bow, you'll be cut.' After she left, I was standing there all alone. And for the first time, I had thought deep down that I have to stand up to this girl - no matter what.

"Upon reaching the hostel, I informed Kushagra about the upcoming meeting of Saurav and Vandana. Both of us then devised a plan for Saurav because he was unaware that Saurav and Vandana would meet that night. We went to meet Saurav and started negotiating. If today we manage to separate you from Vandana, then after meeting Vandana, you'll have to perform all those acts which are considered inappropriate and wrong between a boy and a girl, in front of us. In return, we assure you that we won't tell anyone anything and Vandana bhabhi won't suspect anything.

But you'll have to do all this for the entire year. Hearing all this, Saurabh got up from his bed, walked towards his door and stood there. Both of us (me and Kushagra) were waiting anxiously for Saurabh's response.

We were certain that his answer would be in our favor, but what we wanted to know was which show we would watch. I had bet with Kushagra that no matter what, we'll watch the live show for -

a day, a month, or the entire year (wow!).""The wait finally ended and Mitra began speaking, 'Look, whether you guys are good or bad doesn't concern me.

What you're doing or will do doesn't concern me either. Just now, during the break, Saj and Shahnaaz came to me and informed me about both of your misdeeds and also told me that it was you two who instigated the fight with Vandana.' As Saurabh spoke, both of our eyes widened, and I had only one thought in my mind: what's happening.

While Saurav continued, 'Your transformation was brought about by those two girls, and now there's no need for more nonsense, otherwise I'll showcase such a show in the principal's office that the entire hostel will watch.' Leaving aside Mitra's words, Kushagra grabbed my hand and pulled me towards the rooftop.

I was pressing his head while he was... In our minds, only those two girls were walking, and Kushagra kept asking me the same thing repeatedly, 'Are all girls like this or have their fathers made them special by some special diet?'

And I kept telling Kushagra, 'Our mistake is that we made a deal in front of Mitra and these girls and stooped to do our work, and if you stoop..." Whatever happened happened, but Kushagra's last question once again diverted the mood and provided a new direction. He asked me,

'Everything else is fine, my friend, but where's the knowledge of the chapter now?' And I replied, 'Catch Shahnaaz...'"

TIME TO BE KING OF HELL

"From here onwards, the path I was treading didn't even get approval from my inner self. The journey ahead was so filthy, terrifying, and filled with helplessness that I'd pray no reader of mine walks this path. I wasn't alone; Kushagra was with me. Together, we encountered another person.

A 7-8 year old child was studying in Amit's class, whom we used as a pawn like a news item. Our first target was the warden. With Amit's help, we managed to catch the warden red-handed in the children's maid's room, two or three times. This made it easier for us to demand anything in the hostel.

Just imagine, we were using a movie scene in

real life. Before any items entered the hostel, they were checked by the warden below. Some days, we even earned money by getting questionable items through the children and taking commission. Among these questionable items were alcohol, cigarettes, beer, and marijuana for the kids.

The warden played a dual role in this; he let us go upstairs with the items, and also checked and scolded us. Many times, many kids were caught, and they were punished.

Kushagra had a bad habit of smoking cigarettes, and I was still a complete novice.

One thing both Kushagra and I were puzzled about was what was in this addiction that these kids kept asking for even after being punished. As we kept fulfilling the needs of all the big kids in the hostel, our stature kept growing among all the children. This incident happened on 4th February, which was Kushagra's birthday. Biscuits, chocolates, snacks, and cold drinks were part of our daily routine.

Now the problem was what to do new? While solving this problem, we organized a secret night of intoxication in our room. In this event,

Kushagra's 3 friends were also included. All the intoxicating items were included in this event (alcohol, cigarettes, gutka, marijuana, etc). This was the first moment in life where even I heard a voice from within, warning me not to do anything wrong."

"Disregarding that inner voice, I moved forward. Leaving aside gutka and pan-masala, we indulged in the consumption of every intoxicant. But one thing I couldn't understand that day was why people continue to smoke even when they cough during their initial attempts. Similarly, I couldn't comprehend why people continue to drink beer or alcohol even when it tastes bitter.

Truth be told, the taste of any intoxicant wasn't enjoyable. Whether it was cigarettes, alcohol, or marijuana. In this party we organized, along with Amit, our informant, we made all the small kids in the room consume alcohol, beer, and cigarettes. As a result, the kids danced and slept throughout the night. But everything was fine by morning.

However, as they say, as one indulges, their thoughts become aligned with their actions. This principle applied to both Kushagra and me.

Without words, sometimes it was as if no one could articulate a sentence properly. Occasionally, the consequences were visible even in front of the teacher in class, leading to many apologies and several instances of being restricted from school classes for three days. But the habits didn't diminish.

The entire story beyond this point comprised 15 gallons, as measured by minutes (an average, which was removed by our friends many times). As a result, we had become notorious among thousands of new gallons. And officially, a petition was organized on our hostel floor every week as a part of the 'Best Person of the Week' award. The winner received a 'bottle of drink' for free and had to address the entire floor as 'brother' for a week.

The winner's respect lasted only a week, followed by 'elections' again the next week. Elections were conducted in two phases. After our first phase, the prize was awarded to children aged 6 to 10, with the most swearing and misbehaving kids winning.

The reason behind orchestrating all this among the kids was to prepare the foundation for the upcoming new generation. The hostel environment seemed ideal from a distance; it appeared that all children exercised in the morning, studied together at night, and prayed before starting any activity.

But the reality inside, which I've shared in this chapter, was far from ideal. All these events were happening behind the hostel warden's back; perhaps, nobody could be seen uttering a sentence sometimes.

Occasionally, these repercussions were even seen in front of the teacher in class. Many apologies were made, and several times, we were restricted from attending classes for three days. But the rebellions didn't decrease. The environment was so polluted that despite our attempts to stop such events in our rooms, they continued in other rooms.

The dirt had spread so much that we suspected the hostel warden's involvement in such incidents, but we could never confirm it. Our suspicion persisted until we left the hostel. One thing is certain; no one starts their addiction journey because of the 'taste' of any substance. Either someone is forced into addiction by friends, or some consider these addictions as a symbol of style and fashion, initiating their addiction journey."

"Due to these habits, addiction becomes a lifelong companion. When Kushagra and I instilled addiction in small children, our perspectives differed in this matter. We thought, 'If your parents cannot keep you with them, if they don't have time in their daily routine to educate you, then you have every right to rebel and show your parents how big a mistake they made by leaving you here just to earn money.'

With this thought in mind, we continued forward, becoming the worst and biggest friends in the hostel. I've shared only a few aspects of my journey towards becoming bad and big, just those things that I can easily express in simple words.

But one thing I must emphasize is that upon realization, what I learned was, 'The decision to become the worst from the best.'

MY SILENT LOVE

"Due to our habits, this addiction becomes a lifelong commitment. When I and Kushagra introduced small children to addiction, our thinking was somewhat different in this matter. We used to think that if your parents can't keep you with them, don't have time to educate you, then you have every right to rebel and show your parents how much you've suffered by leaving them and earning money.We both moved forward with this mindset and eventually became the worst in the hostel and the biggest friends in terms of intelligence. I have shared only a few things about my journey to becoming bad and big, just those things that I can tell you in simple words. But one thing I will definitely say is that with the passage of time, my experience has been molded in various ways."

"The journey of the hostel kept going and we

didn't even realize when the year was over. But as soon as the year was over, boys, girls, and teachers started to hate me a little more, because the hostel's worst boy finally reached the top position in the class. Seeing the little hatred for myself, I was also quite happy. The most amusing moment was when Kushagra called me from home and asked, 'Brother, do you have a pass and did he find out that I have topped the class?' Here Kushagra, Rose, and Shahnaz's border exams were over, and our class was in ninth session. After the border exams, when Kushagra, Rose, Shahnaz, and all the children of the 12th border left for home for 3 months, then in those months, my dominance in the hostel increased. Meanwhile, my value in the teachers was also increasing, and here in the hostel, my position was also at its peak. I still remember the day when after the border paper was over, Rose and Shahnaz were also leaving for home with the rest of the 10th children, so I stopped Rose and said to him, 'Take admission somewhere else in 11th, if not, then don't come back home safely.'"

"All those 3 months and the days of our gym holidays passed, so all the children also returned to the hostel. After 2 or 3 days in the hostel, the same atmosphere was created again. Yes, some brothers of the twelfth class were definitely missed. It had been only a few days - I was sitting on my bed humming songs and enjoying my tune when suddenly Kushagra rushed into the room and said, 'Rose and Shahnaz have come back. Their parents have just dropped them off at the gate.' To tell the truth, I was happy then, without fighting with him, those seven or eight days were quite difficult. We both rushed out of the room and started running downstairs. We had just come out of the hostel when we saw both sisters pulling their bags with difficulty towards the Girls' Hostel. After many months, it was the first opportunity when I saw a face filled with pride. I loudly told Kushagra while Rose was listening, 'What if she were there, would she have been so proud then?' Kushagra said, 'When she becomes dark, she can't be proud, my friend, because she doesn't play an ice match with dark colors.'"

"We both laughed heartily. I said to Shahnaz, 'I'll get the bag up from some kid.' We were standing at the gate of our hostel and they were coming towards us. Rose, staring at me, quickly said, 'This time I have come to study from the institute.' I, looking at Kushagra, said while pointing to Rose, 'Friend, I came by car this time. We don't come from 'Jeez' or 'Vid', we are happy to be home.' Saying this, both Kushagra and I burst into laughter. It was the next day - I was sitting in my class when suddenly I was called by a teacher from Rose and Kushagra's class.

The day before, we had planned and stolen all of Rose's pens from Rose's class so that she could never bother him. But where did we know that the opportunity would come again. Upon the teacher's call, I reached the 11th class. I was definitely a little scared that maybe some girls had complained about yesterday's joke.

Finally, when I reached the class, I saw Rose and Shahnaz sitting quietly on their seats, and Kushagra was sitting on his seat smiling. I saw Kushagra smiling like this for the first time, so my fear increased even more - 'Has this boy definitely done something to get me into trouble today?'"

"The teacher proceeded and said, 'Yes, sir.' The teacher said to me, 'Son, tell me how many hours do you study all the children?' I looked at Kushagra and said, '1 to 1:30 hours daily.' The teacher further said, 'Paper time, son.' I said, 'S-s-s-s-sir, 2 hours.'

Then the teacher started and kept listening to the class - 'Look at this boy, this boy studies only 1 hour daily and even during the paper time, only 2 hours, because the rest of the day they have so much work that they don't get time to study.

And all the other work that I make a list of, which they do all day except studying, then they will not get a stamp, maybe they will even get less.' I was continuously staring at Kushagra and silently asking him in my mind - 'What have you done now?'"

The teacher continued speaking. He said, "And listen, all children, some complaints about these princes have been such that whenever they get caught doing something wrong around their bed, they say, 'Sir, my bed was set up to trap me.'"

He went on, "And as for the enemies, their biggest enemy is the floor because it's forbidden to keep items from one building to another, especially near their beds." Upon this statement, all the children burst into laughter and started looking towards Saj. When I looked at Saj, she was also laughing loudly, and then she started staring back at me. The teacher continued speaking without interruption. And the teacher said further, "My dear children, there are some things that I also feel like learning from them, and I also feel like asking them when the warden is against you and complains a lot about you, where do you get the food items to smuggle from?"

The teacher turned towards me and said, "Son, whatever sarcasm you have, you can tell us, because teachers are aware of some demands even from the hostel." While all the children along with me were enjoying this, the teacher didn't stop speaking, and my praises kept increasing.

The teacher continued addressing all the children, "Children, do you all know why, even after saying all this from my mouth, Ajay is still standing next to me? Because today I have something more to tell you all about him. Did you think that this child failed to reach the top position even after studying for 1 hour? And my dear children, you all know that the one who secures the first position, Ajay Hasarna, studies for 5 to 6 hours every day. Today, they will tell you some of their study techniques, and you must learn from all those things."

I was looking towards the class, and my gaze fell on Rose. She was looking at me as if she was waiting to hear what I would say. The teacher stared at me and then tapped his fist towards the bench.

I understood and silently thought to myself, "Son, today just talk about the work because unnecessary things mean punishment." I had just started speaking when Kushagra began explaining, pointing to all of Rose's pens in front of Rose, "Sir, these are her lucky pens, and she has many of them. She secures the first position in class by writing with these pens."

As soon as Rose saw this, she got agitated and exclaimed, "These are my pens, and I need them. Someone has stolen my pens!" The issue shifted to the pens, and some debate ensued. I was scolded and sent back to my class, but the teacher kept the pens with him.

It was July 20th. After those days passed, I never...

We were all sitting together on the hostel roof, chatting as usual. Suddenly, we all started planning something. The essence of the plan was to humiliate Saj (Rose) in some way so that she couldn't dare to look at any of the boys. Under the plan, everyone agreed that as soon as the boys and girls were returning to their hostels after dinner, one of the boys would start arguing with Rose about something, and then all the boys would come together and start shouting at Rose. And seven or eight boys would scold Rose so much that she would break down, and if she complained, all the boys would form a unity. In that unity, all the boys would expose Rose's mistakes. The time for dinner was such a time when all the teachers were also busy with their duties...

The next day. As per the plan, as soon as Rose came forward, Kushagra started speaking to her. As soon as Rose got angry, all the boys came forward, and everyone started speaking out against her. I was at the forefront. Rose was getting agitated, and she started crying. Purushottam approached her and tried to console her. Purushottam was holding her face while Rose trying to free herself.

I couldn't understand what was happening, and I never understood what happened there. Maybe from childhood, I had a habit of respecting every girl, and because of this, I grabbed Purushottam's collar and pushed him away, and I kept saying many abuses to him. When I kept doing this for a while, all my friends left me there and went back to the hostel. Suddenly, Rose pulled my hand and started speaking to me.

I couldn't understand why she was telling me this, and tears came out of my eyes. Then Gent's PTI slapped me and turned me towards the hostel gate. While pushing me, Gent's PTI took me to the hostel gate. After pushing me further, Gent's PTI left me there and went towards the hostel. I sat on the hostel roof for a few hours like that. All my friends were angry with me, and no one was talking to me.

Then around 1:00, Rose came up to the girls' hostel roof. She asked me if I had dinner. I replied, "No." Then she said, "Go down and sleep, it's too late at night." I said, "Yes, you're right, go and sleep." My legs were hanging towards the side of the road from the Girls' hostel gate, and Rose was down there. I was scared. Rose said to me, "Pull your legs back and sit properly, it's not right like this." I remained silent.

"She continued, 'Sorry' from our side, now go down and sleep. I know your friends might be angry with you, but they are wrong, I said 'Sorry' and then she asked me to go down and went to her room downstairs.

Later, she came back upstairs and asked me to go down again. She went down 2-3 times and then again came up after a while. It was around 3:00 or 4:00 in the morning. When night finally fell again, she said to us, 'Okay, don't go down, listen to us, just sit with your legs pulled back.' I asked, 'Are you afraid that I will not go down?' - 'No, it's not like that.'

Then why are you worried about me, you don't even love me? - You're not a bad person. If you stop eating and drinking, you could be the best. Alright, stop talking. - You consider me your enemy? I've been sitting on this roof for the past 6 hours. You came only when someone asked. - First pull your legs back. When we come forward, then we'll talk. Otherwise, we'll finish talking and go down. If you want us to talk, then pull back now. I mean, do you want me to talk to you? Okay, one thing, if I don't go down and don't argue with you, then you will get the answer tomorrow. If you go down now."

START OF AN END

They came like this, into the veins of our hearts, and we kept calling their heart splendid. Something like this happened, the end of this love, that a sea was formed, and floods kept flowing.
Rose: - First, step back, when we talk ahead. Otherwise, we will finish talking and leave. If you want us to talk, step back now.

Me: - It means you want me to talk to you. Okay, one thing, if I don't warn and neither do I, then what?

Rose: - You will get the answer to this tomorrow, if you go down now. Me: - Tomorrow or tonight, because it's already 4:00 in the morning.

Rose: - It's 4 already! Now, because of you, I'll have

to sleep in class. Me: - (laughing) Do you also sleep in class?

Rose: - Why, can't I sleep in class with green eyes? If my color were black, would you still be talking to me at this time?

Me: - First tell me which fair girl in school I talk to nicely? By the way, if you were black, would we have become friends so quickly? :- I'm going to clear you that we are still not friends. We're just talking.

Awake all night till 4:00 in the morning? :-(She cut me off and said, "Why don't you talk at 4:00? But it's important that maybe we're not enemies now. Maybe I was wrong, that you're not dirty-hearted." :- Now go down, we also have to go. The rest of the girls must be waking up. Okay, tell me one thing, do you really study for one hour?

We'll answer this tonight. With this excuse, she turned back, saying "goodnight" while smiling.

- Okay, as you go, let me tell you one secret. You must swear to me not to tell anyone. Shahnaaz likes you. If you have anything for her, I'm here to help you, both. I went to my room and Rose went to her room. As we slept, it was only a minute until the morning exercise bell rang. In the morning exercise, 8 to 10 children from our floor did not go for exercise in the morning.

Because of staying on the roof all night, I also increased my count among those children today. But they say, if there are many benefits of studying, then there are some disadvantages too. Whether it's me or maybe all the children! That day, a ladies PTI came to our hostel with a stick in her hand.

Hearing the loud screams and cries of the children, I understood that today someone is definitely going to get a beating. Even Purushottam and Kuldeep from our room ran out with the group. At first, I thought I would go out with them. But when after a few seconds I heard their cries too, I lay back on my bed as if I hadn't woken up yet. With the ladies PTI stick, she entered the room and came towards my bed.

She screamed 2-3 times and when I didn't get up even after her screams, she pulled me up and said, "Haven't you come down with all the children? Have you stayed here with anyone's permission?"

I said, "I usually go down daily but sometimes I have a problem with my asthma, then I don't go for exercise." She kept her stick aside and sitting on the bed, said, "Okay son, since when?" and putting her hand on my chest, she said, "Son, is it still paining here?" I said, "Yes ma'am, quite fast."

She repeated the same thing again and I again said yes, very fast. After that, the PTI madam gave such a strong slap on my cheek, which I had never seen anyone slap so fast before, nor had I ever been slapped like this.

After that, she pulled me up and started taking me towards the ground assembly with a strong grip, and I was repeatedly thinking in my mind, that what happened suddenly to this PTI madam, which was going well until a while ago, and then suddenly what happened to her.

She stood me up in front of the whole assembly in 1 minute, and narrated the whole incident to all the children. In return, I kept standing firm on my lie, so the madam pressed one side of my chest again and said, "Sorry! Son, is it still paining here?" I felt a little happy from inside and thought whatever happens, a lady teacher apologizing in front of the whole assembly is a matter of pride. And in response to her question, I said, "Yes ma'am, it's still hurting a lot."

The madam made another loud noise in front of the entire assembly, "Hater doesn't happen on the right side, it happens on the left side." The whole assembly burst into laughter and finally, I understood that the matter was about getting slapped, but with severe embarrassment. I looked up and saw Kushagra and Samir along with all the children, laughing, where Rose and Shahnaaz were also present, looking embarrassed.

When the teacher gestured, I joined the line of my classmates. Rose questioned me, 'They sleep the whole night, and even after waking up, they don't come to the guardroom.'

'Parrots,' his comment was teasing. Everything else was fine, but I couldn't understand the parrot part, which I needed to ask about tonight. First, I shared all the night's details with Kushagra, making sure he didn't tell anyone else.

Along with everything else, I also told Kushagra about Shahnaaz's liking. As a result, Kushagra and I decided that from tonight onwards, we would include Shahnaaz in our late-night activities. But another problem emerged in front of Kushagra. You know the saying, 'To catch someone, you have to show them a finger, and the person in front tries to grab the hand.'

We had a similar situation. Since we decided firmly to start the affair with Shahnaaz from tonight, only one thought occupied my mind: tonight's talks shouldn't happen from the boys' hostel roof; they should happen on the girls' hostel roof.

And the solution to this problem was only one person, Mansukh Das, I mean the watchman Mansukh Das. It was evening, and we still didn't know where Mansukh Das's school quarters were. I mean, where he slept during the day because he used to do guard duty all night.

Mansukh Das, we went searching for him inch by inch and finally reached him, but now the attempt to know his weakness has begun. After struggling for some time, it became apparent that Mansukh Das was a big enthusiast for drinking alcohol. Well, what was the big deal, one of our friends got a companion to drink because only two of us among all friends were enthusiasts for drinking alcohol: Baba Bholenath's grace favored one friend and me, the other. Sitting with Mansukh Das first, three glasses of alcohol were downed at his insistence, and then I asked Mansukh Das about his true love.

After finding out all his weaknesses, we also revealed the secrets of our hearts. At first, Mansukh Das seemed to resist a bit, but he bowed before the oath of his true love.

And he said to us, "Son, no one has ever made me this oath until today, that's why I'm helping you, but if you get caught or trapped in any way..." Interrupting him, Kushagra and I said, "Grandpa, if any of us get caught, you should be on top of beating them."

Then I said to Kushagra with a few winks, "Oh..., listen, grandpa, they get worried staying up all night, now it's your job to reach Grandpa's place with alcohol every hour. And who will be providing the pair?"

Kushagra said 'yes' in front of Grandpa, but from behind, he seemed a little annoyed because now he had to stay up all nights without any reason.

And that too with that Grandpa. But a dialogue of friendship convinced him which we always used to say - "This is friendship, this is love, in between is the 'wall of night'.

" Grandpa had the duplicate key of Girls Hostel, which he gave us as a token of trust, saying, "After unlocking the lock, keep the key near the shutter channel of Girls Hostel and when you come back, lock it again. If you get caught, then I'll take the key below and how did you open the lock? You have to find it yourself, without me."

According to the promise, Kushagra and I went to the rooftop only after 10:00 PM. Kushagra sat in a corner of his rooftop, leaning against the wall to hear everything. After quite a while, she came up to the rooftop and started walking without speaking to me. I made some gestures, but there was no response.

I couldn't understand something, then if she came up to the rooftop, why wasn't she talking? It would have been better if she didn't come at all. After some time, I turned back and started heading towards my room. I had reached the rooftop gate when she called from behind - "I couldn't hear her voice and continued towards the gate. But just a little distance away, on the rooftop of Boys Hostel, our friend Garv sat with his hands on his ears.

Kushagra stood up and called out to me, so I stopped at the gate. Garv said, "Hey, where are you going?" Well, what was it, it turned into a mess, the fear of which was there. I kept looking back and forth between Garv and Kushagra. Before I could understand anything, what should I do now? He said - "Will you send her down first?

What is she doing on the rooftop? And if she has been called, why? I find your show-off very ugly." Kushagra replied, "Why are you standing here? :- Meaning still show off. Kushagra said nothing and went downstairs. But he was not less of a master, after all, he was my friend.

He had definitely made a drama of going downstairs, but he stood behind the hostel gate. I moved forward towards Rose and started asking - When you came to the rooftop, why were you ignoring? Were you worried? that Kushagra is sitting here. Rose: Do you know what is my best habit in you?

That I came to meet you. Me: 'What?' Rose- This is that you don't run after any girl from school or hostel. And I think you ignore every girl very quickly. Me: Yes, maybe, because I don't like to bow down. Rose: In front of anyone else? Me: Yes, in front of parents. Rose: I came to the rooftop and saw the same thing, when I ignored, finally how long can you stay up?

And you stopped for only 4 minutes. I like that. I was also thinking the same that although I kept hating this girl from the beginning, but if there was anything I liked, it was not letting any boy harass this girl. I was thinking all this when suddenly Rose said Rose: Now that you have taken the key, why is he standing there? Come. Me: I didn't understand.

Rose: I said don't show off. Me: Uh... uh... alright, I'm coming. Rose: Listen, he will still be standing behind the gate, send him down, there are a lot of mosquitoes on the rooftop (she said laughing) we were going down, just saying to each other - "Where did you learn all this?"

Kushagra: (telling me) Brother, I tell you to go and ask this girl's mother what she ate to give birth to her. Me: (laughing) There's no use, friend, there's only one like that. The other doesn't come.

Kushagra told me to find the key, and then I went towards the rooftop of Girls Hostel after unlocking the lock. Sneaking around, I reached the hostel rooftop, and there Kushagra held the 'bottle' in his hands.

LOVE ZONE

"How do I tell you all about my journey of love that lasted just seven and a half days? The value of these seven and a half days was such that this time became a reason, that I came to live in the world of stars. In these seven and a half days, I learned three types of love and passed through the paths of all three types of love.

I have shared these three types of love with you by giving them the form of three moments. And this is the first moment of our agreement. You must have heard that in an agreement, disagreements are significant, and such an agreement is not fun in which there is no disagreement. So let's embark on the journey of this agreement.

After entering the Girls Hostel, I was heading towards the roof, and for reaching the roof, someone was helping me every day. But one thing was repeatedly revolving in my mind.

Kushagra had told me that brother, you are going to Girls Hostel, but if these two sisters take any action against you or if there is any change in you (caught in Girls Hostel), then let's hug each other one last time. Because then your fate will be in God's hands. In response to Kushagra's words, I said, "If these girls don't harm me, today we are going to become their gods." After a while, I had reached the roof.

She used to come there every day along with me. I went towards one corner of the roof and sat down. She came to me as usual and sat down. - Aren't you afraid? First tell me how did you know about the key thing? - Oh, she was standing by the window in the evening, so I heard the sound of Saurav's conversation.

She was saying to Vandana, why are these Kushagra and his friend hiding? I just assumed from that because I have full faith in your ability in such matters. Without prompting from your mind, how can you come back? - Well, that's all right. This is your new way of talking with a 'you-you' style. I couldn't understand why the 'you' word was used because I was sitting in Girls Hostel. Think about it, maybe you'll use 'you' more than me later. - Oh no! When you're in front of everyone, we should respect you. That's why we call you 'you' in front of everyone, and we'll talk like that. - That's right. The person in front of us calls himself 'me' and me 'you'.

Okay, tell me one thing, will someone doubt that you stayed here all night? - We have a different kind of bond in Girls, and maybe you have a lot of respect in Girls. - Why, I haven't even saved anyone's respect (I said). - No, you haven't saved respect, but many girls say, many times when girls argue with a boy, you pull the boy away. - Maybe, but I didn't pay attention. We were still talking when Shahnaaz came to the roof.

Shahnaaz - Are you both sitting here? By the way, you're sitting in the right place, leave it from somewhere else, even if someone comes to the roof, don't see. Anyway, don't be too scared because there are some girls like this, if any boy goes, they'll find you in your bed. Me - Is it certain what you're saying, that I won't be caught, because if that's the case, then I'll get the lock down from Kushagra.

Shahnaaz - Yes, it's certain, but how will you tell Kushagra? I raised two or three corners from the roof and walked towards Boys Hostel and faced the guard with Kushagra. Kushagra came from there to the road below Girls Hostel, and I signaled him to lock it.

When I was gesturing to lock, Kushagra felt that I was asking if the girls had complained, now what should I do. Kushagra started speaking from below - "No brother, don't lock it. Even a friend won't survive there after getting caught. Brother, please don't lock it, otherwise, I'll have to drink cold water from this bottle for the rest of my life." I signaled Kushagra again and explained the whole thing again.

Kushagra locked and went back to the guard. And I came and sat next to both of them. Daily - So Dada will play this night for the bribe. Me: - No, don't leave anything. Shahnaaz: - Do you like a girl in the hostel? I looked at Shahnaaz and said, "Yes, you." Shahnaaz: - Who, me, or Saj? You, because Saj and I are enemies, we can't even be one. Fate has written in its destiny, and that too without erasing it. :-(Said Shahnaaz) If she doesn't like you, who will you like? Daily) Someone told you that I don't like Shahnaaz. :-(Said Shahnaaz) Shahnaaz, you must have already said yes.

There won't be such a status that you have to propose it first. Or then confirm it whether you love it or not, you will think after proposing. :-(She said to me) Saj is saying it right, I don't have any confirmation yet. Yes, if you propose, maybe I am. Suddenly Shahnaaz said- Go down and see once, there is no problem.

Shahnaaz got up and went downstairs, and my mind was spinning here. I was continuously thinking, why is she hesitating to talk to me finally? And has she sent Shahnaaz down because I don't want to talk to Shahnaaz? I asked myself when I looked in Rose's direction, she was strange. Seeing her, I felt like she wanted to say something to me and was hesitating. Here, I again asked myself a question, does Rose like me?

And if I don't find the answer to this question by my heart, then I asked myself another question, whom do I like, Rose or Shahnaaz? When I closed my eyes to know the answer to this question, I got only one answer 'Roj-Roj-every day'.

When I looked towards Rose again, and held her hands from both wrists and palms, she didn't say anything and was a bit scared. I looked at Rose again and asked for permission. Me: - Can I put my head on your lap? She still didn't say anything and remained silent, and looked down and bowed her eyes. And as I approached to put my head on her head, she did not, but she turned her face in such a way as if my eyes were talking to her squinted eyes, my lips were talking to her cheeks, and my hands held in her hands were also talking to each other.

Despite all this, when she didn't say anything scared, I also consented and touched her both eyes with my both eyes and wanted to get closer, then the proximity increased so much, as if my eyelids were touching her eyelids, her feet with my steps, some splash of her feet with my feet, her hair with my hair, and when the splash of my eyelids with her eyelids.

He shyly turned his face away, and I, too, felt nervous, as if I had just found everything and was making one final effort to find a little more.

That's when Shehnaz climbed up onto the roof and exclaimed, "Shehnaz: Oh God! That's why I wasn't coming down. Now look." The queen was sitting there, sullen and pouting, while this gentleman here seemed restless without them having reconciled. "Alright, both of you, come straight here, and tell me what this argument was all about," Shehnaz said.

After that, Shehnaz took both of our hands, sat us down, and then sat beside us. Then she asked again, "Hey, tell me, why aren't you saying anything? Okay, Sahaj, you tell me what happened?" After she asked this question, I was nervously looking around, and she, looking timid, glanced in my direction. Neither of us had an answer to this question. Shehnaz kept asking questions, and we kept nodding in agreement. After a while, Shehnaz said to Rose, "We're feeling a bit strange, that's why we're staying back to sleep." To Rose, she added, "Okay, it's fine. While Sahaj and I talk a bit more, you go ahead." Rose's facial expressions changed so drastically as if she was not ready to leave me alone on the roof.

Upon hearing Shehnaz's words, Rose moved towards the other corner of the roof. We strolled around for a while, perhaps to feel better. While looking towards Rose, Shehnaz said, "Okay, take a walk, but don't pay attention to us here, because some love and confessions are about to begin."

With this statement, Shehnaz rested her head on my shoulder. At that moment, I could either understand Rose's situation or Rose. Shehnaz's head was on my shoulder, and I kept looking at Rose. Rose's gaze was fixed on my shoulder. I could clearly understand what Rose was going through at that moment, so I stood up and gestured towards Kushagra to open the lock, and then went to Rose and asked her to come down.

She gestured towards Shehnaz with her eyes, as if urging me to take her away. After her gesture, I approached Shehnaz, and before I could say anything, she lowered her head on my shoulder. At that moment, either I could understand Rose's situation or Rose. After her head was on my shoulder, I whispered to Shehnaz, "Hey Shehnaz, let's take her downstairs and tell her what happened." I took Rose down to the gate of the girls' hostel, and she asked me, "Do you like Shehnaz?" I replied, "If I like many girls in the hostel, will you believe me?"

Rose replied, "If we start making noise here, do you know what will happen?" Kushagra was listening to all these things, and upon hearing Rose's noisy remark, he bowed before her and said with a loving gesture, "No, Devi Ji, you don't need to make noise.

He's a straightforward guy who has yet to learn how to talk to girls. I apologize on his behalf." After Kushagra said this, Rose turned towards me and said, "Go, take this addict upstairs, seems like she's overdosed today." Kushagra, giving another taunt to Rose, said to me, "Let's go, Dev Purush, let's go to your room upstairs, and you're fully intoxicated. You've detoxified all the kids in the hostel." After saying this, Rose went up to her room and we went to ours. Kushagra wanted to talk to me before going to bed, but upon my insistence, he went to sleep.

After 2 hours of sleep, as per the schedule, when we reached the class, we felt that our study routine was once again disrupted, and it was.

Most of the time, we slept through the class, and during the breaks, when we stepped out, we saw that Shehnaz and Rose were in the same state as us. However, Rose was there, teaching, writing, and understanding every time we met her. Seeing Rose like this every time, I also silently agreed that Kushagra wasn't wrong. There's something different about this girl, in front of whom we all are useless. After the class ended, we all reached the hostel, and everyone got their sleep.

On waking up in the evening, the same thoughts started swirling in my mind - will Rose come to the roof to meet me tonight or not? I told Kushagra about this dilemma, and he suggested a plan. According to the plan, I had to ask Shehnaz to come to the roof after dinner. Following the plan, Shehnaz came to the roof around 10:00 PM. Even after spending an hour on Shehnaz's roof, when Rose didn't show up, I felt a bit uneasy and understood that I didn't like the events of last night. Even after 2 hours had passed, when Rose didn't come to the roof, I went to the girls' hostel with Shehnaz's help. Some girls knew about my daily visits to the roof.

Vandana had also seen me going towards the roof. Shehnaz sat beside me and kept talking about this topic, how long I had been in love with Shehnaz. But my attention was focused solely on Rose, and I didn't want to come up with any excuses to

Shehnaz.

"I have repeatedly asked Shahnaaz to come upstairs, but she always avoids by saying she's not feeling well. Today, finally, I said to her, 'Shahnaaz, if you don't mind, can we sit here for the next 2 or 3 hours?' Then I told her that I would explain to her tomorrow why I sit alone on the roof every day. After hearing me, Shahnaaz walked away. I sat alone on the roof for half an hour, and then she came up and sat in a corner far from me. I approached her and sat beside her. It was good that from here, we couldn't be seen by anyone. I kept asking her why she didn't come to the roof, and she remained silent, without saying anything.

When she didn't respond for the next half hour, I held her hand and asked her why she didn't come to the roof. In response to my question, she said, 'Every day - Can we claim our right on you, or can you claim your right on us? Think and answer.' I said, 'Yes, of course, why not,' (I said with happiness in my heart) She asked, 'Are you sure?' I said, 'Yes, why not! If we don't recognize ourselves from within, we wouldn't be sitting here. Tell me, what do we need to say, understanding ourselves?'

I was happy inside because I knew that only a few more words about love were about to come. Then, Rose asked me to close my eyes and told me that what she wants to do, she won't be able to do it with my eyes open. I also felt excited, so I started closing my eyes.

While closing my eyes, I felt a slap on my cheek. When I opened my eyes, there was no one around, only Rose was sitting in front of me. Before I could ask her the reason for this, she started crying. When I tried to wipe her tears and make her quiet, I realized that she had a high fever. One thing I forgot to mention was that she had a lot of faith in promises, so I tried to silence her by making many promises and tried to know the reason for the slap. Then she started talking and asked me, 'Rose - If we had a fever today, why did you talk to Shahnaaz for hours after not getting any help? And then you came here to meet her.' She continued, 'Can you talk to Shahnaaz for us?' I said, 'No, no, we can't do that. Don't talk to her anymore.' Then we both became good friends, so I agreed to talk to her only when necessary.

'Okay, I won't talk to Shahnaaz anymore. I promise you.' I said, 'I'll do one more thing for you now.' I told her everything, and then I put my hand on her head. She put her hand on my head. Now you have my promise; you won't do anything for the next 5 minutes; you'll just say it. Then she kept quiet, without saying anything. While waiting for her to say something, I started looking at her. Rose looked surprised, closed her eyes, and looked at me, and after a while, she said two lines while smiling and then came to my hostel, leaving her.

When I was about to leave, she started to ask, "How can I tell you all that my journey of love lasted only for seven and a half days?" The value of these seven and a half days was so much that this alone became a reason, that I came to live in the world of stars.

In these seven and a half days, I learned three types of love and went through the path of all three types of love. I shared with you these three types of love by giving them the form of three moments. And this is the first moment of our agreement.

You all must have heard that there is a big dispute in agreement, and such an agreement is also not fun in which there is no dispute. Let's travel through this agreement. After entering the Girls Hostel, I was going towards the roof, and Rose was also helping me to reach there, but one thing was spinning in my mind repeatedly. Kushagra had told me that brother, you are going to Girls Hostel, but if these two sisters make any move, or if they change their attitude towards you (catch you in Girls Hostel), then embrace your friend for the last time. Because after that, only your God is the owner. In response to Kushagra's words, I said, 'If these girls don't take any step, then today we are going to become their gods.' After a while, I reached the roof. Rose was also coming up with me.

I sat down on the other side of the roof. Rose came and sat beside me. Rose - Aren't you scared? Me - First, tell me how did you know about the key incident? Rose - Oh, she was standing at the window in the evening, so I heard Saurav Mitra's voice. He was saying to Vanshika, why are Kushagra and his friend hiding behind the guard's cabin today? I got an idea from there only because I have complete faith in your abilities in these matters."

"You can convince someone with your heart, how can you come back?

- Okay, everything is fine. I didn't understand this new way of talking, one-on-one.

Why is the word 'you' being used, because I am sitting in Girls Hostel. Think again, even 'you' will be used more than 'you' with me.

- No, man! When you are in front of everyone, we should show respect to you. That's why we call you 'you' in front of everyone, and we will speak like that.

- That's correct. The person in front calls himself 'you' and

me 'you.' Okay, tell me one thing, won't anyone suspect that you stayed here all night?

- We have a different bond in Girls, and maybe you

are respected in Girls. - Why, I haven't even saved

anyone's respect (I said).

- No, you may not have saved respect, but many girls say,

when there have been arguments with boys many times, you take them away.

Maybe, but I didn't pay attention. They were both talking when Shahnaaz came up to the roof.

- Are you both sitting here secretly? Well, you're sitting in the right place, leave from somewhere else too, don't look even if someone comes on the roof from somewhere else. Anyway, don't be too scared because some girls are like that, if a brother goes there, they might hide him in their bed.

- What you're saying is sure, that I won't be caught, because if that happens, I'll get the lock from Kushagra.

- Yes, sure, but how will you tell Kushagra?

I picked up a couple of bricks from the roof and hit the back and front of the boys' hostel with the guard, and towards Kushagra. When Kushagra came up from there and reached the road below Girls Hostel, I gestured to him to lock it. When I was gesturing to lock it, Kushagra felt like I was asking him what to do now. Kushagra started speaking from below - "No brother, don't lock it. Don't hit me. Even my friend won't survive if he is hit from there. Brother please don't hit me otherwise I'll have to drink thick water for life with this bandage." I gestured to Kushagra again and explained the whole thing again, Kushagra locked it and went back to the guard. And I came and sat close to both of them. Rose - So the guard will play rummy in bribery tonight. Me: - No, leave something.

Shahnaaz: - Do you like any girl in the hostel? I turned towards Shahnaaz and said - "Yes, you." Shahnaaz: - Whom, me or Saj?

Me: - You, because Saj and I can't be one, right? Fate has written its law, not to be erased even with ink. Rose: - (said to Shahnaaz) If he doesn't like you, will you like him then? Me: - (to Rose) Someone told me that I don't like Shahnaaz

Rose: - (to Shahnaaz) Shahnaaz, you must have liked him already. There won't be such a status where you have to propose to him first. Or then confirm it whether you love him or not, you will think about it after proposing.

Shahnaaz: - (to me) Saj is right, I don't have any confirmation yet. Then suddenly Rose said to Shahnaaz -

Go down and check, is there any problem? Shahnaaz got up and went downstairs, and my mind was spinning here. I kept thinking, why is she avoiding talking to me? And did she send Shahnaaz down because she doesn't want me to talk to Shahnaaz anymore? Thinking this, when I looked at Rose, she was strange. I felt like she wanted to say something and hesitating.

At this point, I asked myself a question, does Rose like me? And when I closed my eyes to find the answer to this question, I got only one answer 'Roj-Roj-every day'. Then I looked at Rose again and held both of her hands from the sides, she didn't say anything and seemed a little scared. Then I asked Rose for permission.

Can I put my head on your head?

She still didn't say anything and looked down and bowed her head, and I also moved a little forward to bring her face closer, then she didn't touch my head, but she turned her face a bit as if my eyes were talking to her eyes, my lips were talking to her cheeks, and my hands were talking to her hands, even then when she hesitated and didn't say anything, I also hesitated and tried to bring both her eyes closer to mine, the closeness increased so much, as if my eyelashes were touching her eyelashes, my hands were held by her hands, her hair was intertwined with mine, and as soon as the touch of my eyelashes touched her eyelashes, an excited touch happened on our faces, as if she had turned away a bit after a while, neither was she looking at me nor me.

She shyly turned her face away and I was also lost as if everything was found just now and I was trying to get a little more, then Shahnaaz came upstairs and said - Shahnaaz: - Oh God! That's why I wasn't going down. Now see

She is sitting there like a queen, her face is hidden, and these gentlemen are fighting without any peace. Come straight down now

and tell me why you two fought now. After this, Shahnaaz grabs both our hands and makes us sit straight and sits next to us. And then she asks - Shahnaaz: - Tell me, tell me why you're not saying anything? Okay Saj, first you tell me what happened?

Here's the translation of the provided text from Hindi to English:

"After asking him that, I was looking towards the ground with a hesitant glance, and she, too, looked at me hesitantly. Neither of us had an answer to this question. Shahnaz kept asking, and we kept agreeing. After some time, Rose and Shahnaz said, 'Rose: - (to Shahnaz) We're feeling a bit strange, so we're going to sleep. Shahnaz: - (to Rose) Okay, you go, we'll talk more until then. Rose's expression changed so much that it seemed like she didn't want to leave me alone on the roof.

After Shahnaz said this, Rose went towards the other corner of the roof and said, 'Rose: - Let's spend some time on the roof for a while, maybe we'll feel better.' (Looking at Rose) Okay, let's take a stroll, but don't pay attention to us because some love and confession matters are about to begin here.' (Shahnaz said this, resting her head on my shoulder) At that time, I could understand Rose's discomfort very well, so I got up and gestured towards the lock, indicating to open it. Then I went to Rose and asked her to let me down, she gestured towards Shahnaz with her eyes as if telling me to take her down.

After this gesture, I had moved towards Shahnaz, but I heard Rose's voice from behind: - 'Shahnaz, we'll bring this down and come back to tell you what happened. Rose brought me down to the gate of the girls' hostel and asked me: - 'Do you like Shahnaz? If I like many girls in the hostel, will you make my talk known to everyone?'

If we start making noise here, who knows what will happen? Kushagra was standing with us at the gate listening to all these things, and when he heard Rose's noise-making comment, he bowed in front of Rose, clasped his hands, and said with affection, 'No, Devi Ji, there is no need to make noise.

This is an outspoken person who has not yet learned to talk to girls properly. I apologize on his behalf.' After Kushagra said this, Rose turned towards me and said, 'Rose: - Go, take this addict upstairs, it seems she's overdosed today.' Kushagra gave another taunt to Rose and said to me, 'Let's go, Dev Purush, let's go upstairs to our room, and you are totally intoxicated.

You have freed all the kids of the hostel from addiction.' After hearing Kushagra's comment, Rose went upstairs to her room, and we went to ours.

Kushagra wanted to talk to me before going to bed, but on my insistence, he went to sleep, and I went to mine. After sleeping for 2 hours, when we reached the class according to the schedule, we felt that our way of studying was once again getting disorganized, and that's what happened. Most of the time, the teacher was sleeping through his class.

In between classes, when we went out a couple of times, we saw that Shahnaz and Kushagra were in the same condition as us. However, Rose met us every time, reading, writing, and understanding. Seeing Rose like this every time, I was also silently acknowledging that Kushagra wasn't wrong - there's something different about this girl, in front of whom we all are worthless.

After the class ended, we all reached the hostel, and everyone got their sleep. In the evening, when I woke up, the same thoughts started swirling in my mind - will Rose come to meet me on the roof tomorrow or not? When I told Kushagra about this dilemma, he suggested something. According to the plan, I had to ask Shahnaz to come to the roof after dinner.

Following the plan, Shahnaz arrived around 10:00 at night. Even after spending a full hour on Shahnaz's roof, when Rose didn't show up, I also began to feel anxious and understood that I was feeling bad about last night's events. Even after 2 hours had passed, when Rose didn't come to the roof, I sought Shahnaz's help and went to the hostel's terrace.

Where we had sat yesterday, I sat down and Shahnaz came to me. Some girls knew about my daily visit to the roof."

Rose had already seen me looking towards the

rooftop. She continued to sit beside me, talking about how long I had loved Shehnaz. But my focus was solely on Shehnaz, determined not to be swayed by mere words and everyday occurrences.

I had asked Shehnaz several times to come upstairs, but she always diverted the conversation by citing some excuse about her health. Finally, I mustered the courage and said to her, "Shehnaz, if you don't mind, can you sit here with me for the next 2 or 3 hours?" Then I also told her that I would tell her tomorrow the reason for wanting her to sit on the rooftop with me. Upon hearing my words, Shehnaz went downstairs.

For half an hour, I sat alone on the rooftop, and then half an hour later, Shehnaz came up to the roof again and sat in a corner away from me. I approached her and sat beside her. It was good that from here, no one could see us. I kept asking her why she didn't come to the rooftop. She remained silent, without saying anything. When she didn't respond for the next half an hour, I held her hand and asked her why she didn't come to the rooftop. In response, she said to me, "Can we claim ownership of you, or do you belong to yourself?

Think about it and give an answer." I replied inwardly, "Yes, why not?" outwardly saying, "Absolutely, why not! If we didn't recognize ourselves from within, we wouldn't have been sitting here, right? Tell me, what should I say, understanding myself?" Internally, I was happy because I knew that there were three letters of love coming from her side. Then I eagerly awaited those words. Rose asked me to close my eyes and told me that what she wanted to do, she wouldn't be able to do it with my eyes open. Excitedly, I closed my eyes.

While waiting, I felt uneasy, and suddenly, I felt a slap on my cheek. When I opened my eyes, there was no one around except Rose, who was sitting in front of me. Before I could ask her the reason, she started crying. When I tried to wipe her tears and make her quiet, I realized that she had a high fever.

One thing I forgot to mention was that she had a lot of trust in promises, so after making several promises and trying to make her quiet, when I tried to find out the reason for the slap, she started talking about Shehnaz and me. Then she asked me, "If we had a fever today, why did you talk to Shehnaz for hours by calling her to the rooftop? And then you came here to meet her?" I replied, "Yes, I will try to talk to Shehnaz for us, but only when it's necessary." She said, "No, no, don't talk to her unnecessarily. We are such good friends now that you shouldn't even think of talking to her.

Now that we have become such good friends, you should listen to me."

I said, "Alright, I won't talk to Shehnaz ever. I promise. Yes, I'll do one more thing for you right now." She asked, "What?" I said, "I'll tell you everything," and I extended my hand and placed it on my forehead. Rose put her hand on my forehead.

I said, "Now, you have my promise, for the next 5 minutes, neither will you do anything nor say anything." Then she remained silent, without saying anything. I looked at her expectantly, waiting for her to say something. When I had made Rose swear at that time, Shehnaz had come to the rooftop and sat beside us. Rose also kept glancing at me curiously, trying to figure out what "Saj" was about to say.

I grabbed Rose's wrist with my right hand and, moving my left hand toward her head, held it for a while like this, coming so close to her that her hair mingled with mine, her eyes met mine, her face touched mine, and her lips touched mine. After a few moments like this, I backed away. Rose looked surprised, blinking and looking at me, while Rose and I, smiling, said two such lines to each other and then went back to our hostel, which must have echoed in her ears even after I left. When I was about to leave, I said to Rose while looking back, "Don't call me a friend next time, because we are not friends anymore. Love you, love you, and you love me, me, me, 'Roj-Roj-Har-Roj'.

"How do I tell you all that my journey of love lasted just seven and a half days. The price of these seven and a half days was so high that this alone became the reason, for which I came to live in the world of stars. In these seven and a half days, I learned three types of love and passed through the paths of all three types of love. I have shared these three types of love with you by giving them the form of three moments.

And this first moment is our agreement. You must have heard that there is a big argument in agreement, and such an agreement is also not interesting in which there is no argument. Let's travel through this argument. After entering Girls Hostel, I was heading towards the roof, and she was helping me every day to reach the roof, but one thing was repeatedly revolving in my mind.

Kushagra had told me that brother, you are going to Girls Hostel, but if these two sisters play any trick or do anything to you (catch you in Girls Hostel), then hug your friend for the last time.

Because afterward, only your god will be your owner. In response to Kushagra's words, I said, 'If these girls don't catch me, then today we are going to become their gods.' After a while, I reached the roof. She was reaching there along with me every day. I went towards a corner of the roof and sat down. She came and sat beside me as usual. Every day she asks, 'Aren't you afraid?' I replied, 'First tell me how did you know the key to the Girls Hostel's duplicate lock?' She said, 'Oh, she was standing at the window in the evening, so I heard Saurav's voice. He was saying to Vanshika, why are these Kushagra and his friend hiding?

I understood from that because I have full confidence in your capability in such matters.' Without convincing your mind, how can you come back? I said, 'Okay, everything is fine, but I didn't understand your new way of talking in tu-tu.' Meaning, why is the word 'you' being used, because I am sitting in Girls Hostel. Think, you won't even be called 'you' more than me.

She said, 'No! When you are in front of everyone, we should respect you. That's why we call you 'you' in front of everyone, and we will say that way. I said, 'That's right. The person in front calls himself 'we' and me 'you'. Okay, tell me, will anyone doubt where you were when you stayed here all night?'

She replied, 'We have a different kind of bond in Girls, and maybe you won't have respect in Girls,. I said, 'Why, I didn't even save anyone's respect even when it was being looted (I said).'

'No, you didn't save respect, but many girls say,

when there have been arguments between girls and boys, then you pull him away from there.' Maybe, but I didn't pay attention. Both were still talking when Shahnaaz came to the roof. 'Are you both sitting here?' She said. 'By the way, you are sitting in the right place, leave it somewhere else too, don't even look if someone else comes on the roof.' By the way, don't be too scared because some girls are like this, if a brother goes, then they put you in their bed.

'What you are saying is true that I won't be caught,' because if it is, then I will lock Kushagra downstairs.' 'Yes, it is true, but how will you tell Kushagra?' I raised a couple of kicks from the roof, and with the guard of the boys' hostel and looking towards the front, I gestured towards Kushagra.

When I was gesturing to lock, Kushagra felt that I was asking if the girls had complained, what should I do now, he started saying from below, 'No brother, don't lock. Don't even shake it, otherwise, the friend will also not survive if you shake it from there. Please don't shake it, otherwise, with this headache, I will have to drink a bucket full of cold water in jail.' I gestured to Kushagra again and explained the whole thing again, Kushagra locked and went back to Dadda. And I came back and sat with these two."

"So, Dadda will drink all night in bribe. No, don't leave anything. :- "Do you like any girl in the hostel? Looking at Shehnaz's face, he said- "You"

Shehnaz: - "Who, me or Saj? Me: - "You, because Saj and I are enemies, right, we can't even be one" - Destiny has written in its own way, without erasing with ink. Every day: - (said to Shehnaz) If she doesn't like you, will you like her?

Me: - (from Shehnaz) Who said I don't like Shehnaz?

Every day: - (said to Shehnaz) Shehnaz must have said yes to you before. There won't be such a status that you have to propose to her first.

Or else understand it properly before proposing, whether you love her or not, you will think after proposing. Shehnaz: - (said to me) This is what Saj is saying right, I have no commitment right now. Yes, if you propose to me, maybe I can. Then suddenly Rose said to Shehnaz- "Shehnaz, come down and see, is there any problem?" Shehnaz got up and went down and my mind was spinning here.

I was constantly thinking why she sent Shehnaz downstairs to talk to me? And did she send Shehnaz downstairs because I didn't talk to her? While thinking this, when I looked at Rose, she was strange. She felt as if she wanted to say something to me and was hesitating. At this point, I asked myself a question, does Rose like me? And if I didn't find the answer to this question by my mind, I asked myself another question, who do I like, Rose or Shehnaz?

When I closed my eyes to find the answer to this question, I only got one answer 'Everyday'. I looked at Rose again and held both her hands and wrists. She didn't say anything and was slightly nervous. Then I asked Rose for permission again. Can I keep my head on your head? She still didn't say anything and looked down and bowed her head. And as I approached her to put my head on hers, she didn't touch my head, but turned her face slightly, as if my eyes were talking to her half-closed eyes, my lips were talking to her cheeks, and when the splash of my eyelids touched her eyelids, then an excited splash happened on our faces, as if she had turned back a few moments later.

Neither was she looking at me nor was I. She looked shy and turned her face back and I was also shy as if I had just found everything and was just trying to get a little more, then Shehnaz went upstairs to the roof and said- Oh God! That's why I wasn't going down. Now see, she is looking up there, sitting with a full mouth and these sir are not leaving each other, unable to sleep. Let's go both of you straight and let's see.

After this, Shehnaz held both of our hands and sat us straight and we sat close to each other. Then she asked again- tell me, why aren't you speaking? Okay Saj, you tell me what happened first? After asking this, I was nervous towards Rose and she was looking at me with soft eyes. Neither of us had an answer to this question. Here, Shehnaz kept asking and we kept nodding. After a while, Rose and Shehnaz said- We are feeling a little strange, so we are going to sleep.

Rose: - (towards Shehnaz) Okay, let's go, but listen, don't pay attention to us because something love and confession is going to start here (Shehnaz said this and had put her head on my shoulder) At this time, Rose's head was on my shoulder, I was constantly looking at Rose. Rose's eyes were fixed on my shoulder.

At that time, I could understand Rose's discomfort very well, so I got up and signaled Rose and some gestures to unlock and said, go down. Then I went to Rose and asked her to let me down, she gestured towards Shehnaz with her eyes as if she was saying, go and take her.

After this gesture of hers, I had taken a few steps towards Shehnaz when Rose's voice came from behind - Rose: - Shehnaz, let's drop it down and come back and tell us what fight happened with it."

Here is the translation of the text from Hindi to English:

"Rose brought me down to the hostel gate and asked me, 'Do you like Shehnaz? If I like many girls in the hostel, will you get me married?' :- Now if we start making noise here, who knows what will happen?

Kushagra was standing at the gate listening to all these things and when he heard Rose's noisy talk, he bowed his hands in front of Rose and said sarcastically, 'No Devi ji, there is no need for you to make noise. He is an outspoken person and he still hasn't been able to understand that girls should not be teased. I apologize to you on his behalf."

On hearing Kushagra say this, Rose turned towards him and said, "Go take this drunkard upstairs, it seems he's overdosed today. Come, Dev Purush, let's go to your room upstairs, and you are completely drunk. You have made all the children of the hostel sober."

After hearing this taunt from Rose, she went to her room and we to ours. Kushagra wanted to talk to me before sleeping, but on my refusal, he went to sleep and I... After sleeping for a few hours, when we reached class according to our schedule, we felt that our way of studying was once again becoming disorganized, and that's exactly what happened. Most of the time, we completed our sleep by hiding from the teacher.

When we came out of class two or three times in between, we saw that Shehnaz and Kushagra were in the same condition as us. But Rose was seen studying, writing, and understanding every time. Seeing Rose like this every time, I was also silently scolding myself and thinking that Kushagra is not wrong.

There is something different in this girl, before whom we all are useless. After the end of the class, we all reached the hostel and everyone completed their sleep. On waking up in the evening, the same thoughts started swirling in my mind, what will happen after yesterday?

Will Rose come to meet me on the roof or not? When I told Kushagra about this problem, he suggested something. According to the plan, I had to ask Shehnaz to come to the roof after having dinner. Shehnaz came to the roof around 10:00 at night as planned. Even after Shehnaz was on the roof for a whole hour, when Rose did not come to the roof, I also felt a little worried and understood that Rose did not like the antics of last night. Even after two hours had passed, when Rose did not come to the roof, I went to the hostel roof with Shehnaz's help.

Where we sat yesterday, I sat there and Shehnaz came to me. Some girls knew about my daily visits to the roof. Even Vandana had seen me coming towards the roof. Shehnaz sat next to me and kept talking to me about how long I had been in love with her. But my attention was focused only on Shehnaz, ignoring Rose's absence. I asked Shehnaz several times to call her up, but she said Rose was feeling unwell and changed the subject.

Finally, I said to Shehnaz, 'Shehnaz, if you don't mind, can I sit here for the next 2 or 3 hours?' and then I also told Shehnaz that I would definitely tell her the reason for my sitting alone on the roof tomorrow. After hearing my words, Shehnaz went downstairs.

For half an hour, I just kept sitting alone on the roof like this, and then after half an hour, Rose came to the roof and sat far away from me. I got up and went to her and sat down next to her. Well, it was good that we were not visible to anyone from here. For a long time, I kept asking her why she didn't come to the roof and she kept sitting silently without saying anything.

When she didn't give me any answer even after the

next half hour, I held her hand in mine and asked her why she didn't come to the roof. In response to my question, she said to me, 'Can we assert our right over you or do you belong to us? Think and answer.'"

"Yes, why not?" (he said happily to himself) "Absolutely, right? Yes, why not go crazy! If we don't accept ourselves from the inside, we wouldn't sit here. Tell me, what do I need to tell you, understanding myself? I was secretly happy because I knew that the two and a half letters of love are about to come from ahead. And then I started looking forward to those words with a smile. Rose used to tell me to close my eyes every day and told me that what she wanted to do, she wouldn't be able to do it with my open eyes.

I, too, felt encouraged and closed my eyes. As I was closing my eyes, I felt a slap on my cheek. When I opened my eyes, there was no one around, just Rose sitting in front. Before I could ask her the reason for this, she started crying. When I tried to wipe her tears and make her quiet, I realized that she had a high fever.

One thing I forgot to tell you is that she had a lot of trust in promises, so after giving her many promises and trying to make her quiet, I wanted to know the reason for the slap. Then she started all over again, and then she asked me, 'Do you want to talk to Shahnaaz for me?'

Me: - Yes, I will try to talk to her only when the time comes. Rose: - No-no, we are not. Don't talk to her beyond what you need to say. Now that we have become such good friends, you should listen to us too.

I: - Okay, I won't talk to Shahnaaz. I swear to you. Yes, I'll do one more thing for you right now.

Rose: - "What?" I: - I'll tell you everything. And she reached out and put her hand on my head. Rose put her hand on my head.

I: - Now it's your turn, you won't do or say anything for the next 5 minutes. Then she became silent without saying anything and kept looking at me waiting for me to say something. When I had asked Rose to take this oath, at the same time Shahnaaz came to the terrace and started sitting near us.

Shahnaaz was telling me that she was wondering what Saj is going to say. I grabbed Rose's wrist with my right hand and moved my left hand towards her head, pulling her closer to me for a while, so close that her hair was touching mine, her eyes were looking into mine, her face was close to mine, and her lips were touching mine. After a few moments of staying like this, I moved back.

Shahnaaz looked surprised, blinked her eyes and was looking at me, and to some extent, Rose was also looking at me smiling, and I, smiling, said two such lines to Rose and went back to my hostel, which must still be ringing in her ears even after I left. When Rose was leaving after talking to me, I said to her, "Don't call me a friend next time, because we are not friends anymore, love you - love you, and you love me - me - me - 'Roj-roj-every day.'

How should I tell you all that my journey of love was just for seven and a half days? The price of these seven and a half days was so high that it became a reason, that's why I came to live in the world of stars. I learned three types of love in these seven and a half days and passed through the paths of all three types of love. I have shared with you all three types of love by giving them the form of three moments.

And this is the first moment of our agreement.

You must have heard that there is a big argument in agreement, and such an agreement is also not fun in which there is no argument. After entering Girls, Hostel, I was going towards the terrace, and Rose was also helping me, but a word was wandering in my mind repeatedly.

Kushagra had told me that brother, you are going to Girls, Hostel, but if these two sisters do something, or if you get caught or something changes in you (by catching in Girls Hostel), then hug the friend for the last time. Because after that, only your god is the lord. In response to Kushagra's words, I said - "If these girls do anything wrong, then today we are going to become their god." After a while, I had reached the terrace. Rose had also reached there with me.

I went towards one side of the terrace and sat down. Rose came to me and sat down. - Aren't you scared? First tell me how did you come to know about the key? You have taken the duplicate key of the hostel gate. - Oh, she was standing by the window in the evening, so I heard Sourav's voice.

He was saying to Vandana why these Kushagra and his friend are hiding? I just guessed from that why are they hiding? In these matters, I have complete faith in your capability. Without expressing your mind, how will you come back? - Okay, that's right.

The word 'you' is being said because I am sitting in Girls, Hostel. Imagine that you will not even say 'you' to me more than once. Rose - No, no! When you

Here's the translation of the text from Hindi to English:

"Wouldn't there be such a status that you wouldn't have to propose first? Or rather, understand it first whether you love it or not, think about it after proposing." :-(She said to me) This thing is being said right.

Right now, I don't have any confirmation. Yes, if you propose, maybe I would. Suddenly, Rose said to Shahnaaz - "Shahnaaz, go downstairs once and see, there's no problem."

Shahnaaz got up and went downstairs, and my mind was spinning here. I kept thinking why is Rose spinning me around when I'm about to talk to Shahnaaz?

And did she send Shahnaaz downstairs because she didn't want me to talk to Shahnaaz? Thinking this, when I closed my eyes to know the answer to this question, I got only one answer 'Roj-Roj-Har Roj'. I looked at Rose again and held both her wrists with my hands. She didn't say anything and seemed a bit nervous.

Then I asked Rose for permission. Me: - Can I lay my head on your lap? She still didn't say anything and lowered her eyes, and I, being a bit nervous, brought her eyes down with mine, trying to bring her closer by placing my head on hers, as if my eyes were talking to hers, my lips were talking to her cheeks, and my hands held hers.

But even then, when she didn't say anything nervously, I, too, agreeing, tried to bring her eyes closer to mine by touching both her eyes with mine a little more, and our proximity increased so much that it seemed as if my eyelashes were touching hers, my hands were holding hers, and some sparks were felt between our footsteps and her hair with my footsteps, her face was turned slightly as if she was talking to my eyes with her half-closed eyes, her lips were talking to my cheeks, and my hands were talking to hers.

Despite all this, when she didn't say anything nervously, I also, in agreement, touched both her eyes with mine and tried to get a little closer, but when she still didn't say anything, I also agreed and moved her eyes from both my shoulders to her cheeks a bit more, and she also turned her face slightly as if she was trying to hold me tighter on the roof and not let me go.

When Shahnaaz said this, Rose went to the other corner of the roof, holding my hand, and sat down. She then asked - "Hey, tell me, why aren't you saying anything? Okay, Saj, you tell me first, what happened?" After she asked this, looking at Rose, I was feeling nervous, and she was looking back at me nervously.

Neither of us had an answer to this question. Shahnaaz kept asking here, and we kept agreeing. After a while, Rose said to Shahnaaz - :-(looking at Rose) We're feeling a bit strange, so we're staying silent. :-(to Rose) Okay, fine, you go on talking while we take some rest.

Rose's facial expressions changed so much that it seemed she didn't want to leave us alone on the roof. On Shahnaaz's saying this, Rose, looking at the other corner of the roof, said - "Let's take a little stroll on the roof, maybe it'll feel good. Shahnaaz: -(Looking at Rose and then at me) Okay, take a stroll, but listen, don't pay attention to us here because some love and confession talks are about to start here now. (Shahnaaz said this, laying her head on my shoulder) At this time, I could understand Rose's condition, or Rose.

Shahnaaz's head was on my shoulder, and I was continuously looking at Rose. Rose's gaze was fixed on my shoulder. Rose's condition at that time I could understand well, so I got up and gestured to Kushagra to open the lock. Then I went to Rose and asked her to go downstairs. She signaled to Shahnaaz with her eyes, as if she was insisting to take her down.

After this signal from her, I went near Shahnaaz and asked her to go down. Then I went to Rose and asked her to go down, and she asked me with her eyes to take Shahnaaz up. After this signal from her, I asked Shahnaaz to go up with me, and Rose told Shahnaaz while gesturing to me - "Shahnaaz, we leave it down and tell him what happened with us. Rose brought me downstairs to the gate of Girls, Hostel, and she asked me -

Rose: - Do you like Shahnaaz?

Me: - If I like many girls in the hostel, will you fulfill my wish?

Rose: - Now if we start making noise here, you know what will happen? Kushagra was listening to all these things standing at the gate, and when he heard Rose's noisy talk, he folded his hands and bowed his head, saying, "No, Devi ji, you don't need to make noise here. This is an outspoken person, and he has never been able to understand till date that he should talk to girls. I apologize to you on his behalf." Saying this, Kushagra turned to Rose and said, "Go take this intoxicated man upstairs, it seems like he's overdosed today.

You've made all the boys in the hostel drug-free."

Here's a translation of the text you provided:

"Listening to this taunt every day, I got up angrily and went to my room, and we went our separate ways. Kushagra wanted to talk to me before going to sleep every day, but upon my refusal, he went to sleep, and I ... After sleeping for an hour, according to the daily routine, when we reached the class, we felt that our way of studying was again becoming disorganized, and the same happened. Most of the time, we slept through the teacher's lectures. During class breaks, two or three times when we went out of our class, we saw that the condition of Shahnaz and Kushagra was similar to ours.

But every day, seeing this, I was secretly admitting that Kushagra is not wrong - there is something different about this girl, in front of whom we are all useless. After the class ended, we all reached the hostel and everyone slept. On waking up in the evening, the same thought started revolving in the mind, whether she would come to meet on the roof tomorrow or not? I told Kushagra about this problem, so he suggested something. According to the suggestion, I had to ask Shahnaz to come to the roof after dinner. As per the plan, Shahnaz came to the roof around 10:00 at night.

Even after an hour of being on Shahnaz's roof, when she did not come to the roof the next day, I also became anxious in my mind and understood that the actions of last night have made Rose feel bad.

Even after two hours, when Rose did not come to the roof, I went to the roof of the girls' hostel with Shahnaz's help. Where we had sat yesterday, I sat there and Shahnaz came to me. Some girls knew about my daily coming to the roof. Vandana had also seen me coming towards the roof. Shahnaz kept talking to me about this while sitting next to me. I had been loving Shahnaz for so long, but my attention was only on Rose.

I asked Shahnaz several times to call her upstairs, so she turned the conversation by saying that Rose was not feeling well today. After listening to me, Shahnaz went downstairs. For half an hour, I sat alone on the roof like this, and then after half an hour, when Rose did not come, I asked Shahnaz for help and went to the roof of the girls' hostel. Where we were sitting yesterday, I went there and sat down and Shahnaz came to me. Some girls had seen us coming to the roof. Shahnaz was sitting next to me. On seeing Shahnaz, I started talking to her about what I had been repeating in my mind. Shahnaz kept looking at me with curiosity, and to some extent, Rose was also curious about what 'Saj' was going to say.

I grabbed Rose's wrist with my right hand and extended my left hand towards her, holding her head in my hands for a while, holding her so close that her hair was intertwined with mine, her eyes with mine, her face with mine, and her lips with mine. After a few seconds of staying like this, I moved back. Shahnaz was surprised, staring at me with her eyes wide open, and Rose was smiling. And while smiling, Rose said two such lines to me and came back to her hostel after me, which must have been echoing in her ears even after I left. When Ro\se was about to leave, I told Rose-

Me: - "Next time, don't call me a friend, because we are not friends anymore. I love you - I love you, and you love me - me- me- 'Roj-Roj-everyday'. How should I tell you that my love journey lasted for only seven and a half days? The price of these seven and a half days was so high that this became a reason, that we were going to become their gods today.

Kushagra had told me that brother, you are going to the girls' hostel, but if these two sisters take any step, or change you in any way (catch you in the girls' hostel), then hug your friend for the last time.

Because after that, your god will be only you. In response to Kushagra's words, I said - "If these girls didn't accept, then today we are going to become their gods." After a while, I reached the roof. Rose was helping me to reach the roof, but Kushagra's words were revolving in my mind.

Kushagra had said to me - "Brother, you are going to the girls' hostel, but if these two sisters take any step, or change you in any way (catch you in the girls' hostel), then hug your friend for the last time. Because after that, your god will be only you."

In response to Kushagra's words, I said - "If these girls didn't accept, then today we are going to become their gods." After a while, I reached the roof. Rose was helping me to reach the roof, but Kushagra's words were revolving in my mind.

Kushagra had said to me - "Brother, you are going to the girls' hostel, but if these two sisters take any step, or change you in any way (catch you in the girls' hostel), then hug your friend for the last time. Because after that, your god will be only you." In response to Kushagra's words, I said - "If these girls didn't accept, then today we are going to become their gods." After a while, I reached the roof. Rose was helping me to reach the roof, but Kushagra's words were revolving in my mind."

Here's the translation of the text you provided:

"Rose also arrived there with me. I went towards the corner of the roof and sat down. Rose came and sat beside me.

- Aren't you afraid? First tell me, how did you find out about the hostel's duplicate key?

- Oh, when Vrinda was standing at the window in the evening, I heard Sourav's voice. He was asking Vrinda why Kushagra and his friend were lingering around the security guard's cabin? I just guessed from that because I trust your capabilities in these matters. Without guiding you, how can you come back?

- Well, that's okay. I didn't understand your new way of talking, like constantly addressing me as 'you.' Meaning, why is the word 'you' being used, because I'm sitting in the girls' hostel. Imagine, 'you' will be used even more than me.

- Oh no! When you're in front of everyone, we should show respect. That's why we call you 'you' in front of everyone, and that's how we'll speak.

- That's right. The person in front speaks 'you' to himself and 'me' to me. Okay, tell me one thing, won't anyone doubt if you stay here all night?

- We have a different kind of bond in the girls' hostel, and perhaps you don't realize that you have quite a bit of respect in the girls' hostel. - Why, I didn't even save anyone's respect even after plundering it (I said).

Rose - No, you didn't save respect, but many girls say that when there have been arguments with boys several times, you pull the boy away. Me - Maybe, but I didn't pay attention. We were still talking when Shahnaz came to the roof.

Shahnaz - Are you both sitting here huddled together? By the way, you're sitting in the right place, don't look elsewhere, even if someone else comes to the roof. Also, don't be too scared, because some girls are such that if any guy goes there, they might find him in their bed. Me - Is what you're saying confirmed? That I won't get caught because if that's the case, then I'll put a lock on Kushagra.

Shahnaz - Yeah, that's confirmed, but how will you tell Kushagra? I picked up a couple of bricks from the roof and hit the security guard's cabin below the boys' hostel and then went down in front of Kushagra.

When Kushagra came from there to the road below the girls' hostel, I signaled him to put the lock. When I was signaling to put the lock, Kushagra felt like I was asking him if the girls had complained, what should I do now? Kushagra started speaking from below - "No brother, don't put the lock.

Your friend won't even have bones left if he's caught there. Please don't put the lock, otherwise I'll have to drink water in the middle of the night with this duffel bag." I signaled to Kushagra again and explained the whole thing again.

Kushagra locked it and went back to the duffel bag. And I sat down with these two again. Rose - So, Dadda will play in bribe all night. Me: - No, leave some. Shahnaz: - Do you like any girl in the hostel? I looked at Shahnaz and said - "Yes, you." Shahnaz - To whom, to me or Saj? You, because S

aj and I are enemies, right, we can't be one. Destiny has written this in its own way, not even to be erased. :-(Saying to Shahnaz) If she doesn't like you, then whom will she like? (From Rose) Someone told me that I don't like Shahnaz. :-(From Shahnaz) Shahnaz, you must have already known.

There won't be such a status where you have to propose first. Or else confirm it whether you love it or not, after proposing this thing, you'll think. :-

(Said to me) Saj is saying it right, I don't have any feelings right now. Suddenly, Rose said to Shahnaz - Go downstairs once and see, if there's no problem. Shahnaz got up and went downstairs, and my mind was spinning here.

I kept thinking constantly, why is she hesitating to talk to Shahnaz? And has she sent Shahnaz downstairs so that I don't talk to her. While thinking this, when I looked at Rose, she was strange. It felt like she wanted to say something to me and was hesitating. Here I asked myself again, does Rose like me? And when I closed my eyes to find the answer to this question, I only found one answer 'Roj-Roj-every day'. I looked at Rose again and grabbed both her wrists and hands from her elbows and palms. She didn't say anything to this, and seemed a little nervous. Then I asked Rose for a command."

Here's the translation of the text you provided from Hindi to English:

I: Can I rest my head on your head? She still didn't say anything, and remained silent, lowering her eyes. And as I moved forward a bit, putting my head on hers and bringing our faces closer, she turned her face slightly as if my eyes were speaking to hers, my lips were talking to hers, and my hands held hers, conversing with each other.

Despite all this, when she still didn't say anything, I, too, hesitantly tried to bring her eyes closer to mine. The intimacy increased so much that it felt as if my eyelids were touching hers, and as soon as the touch of my eyelashes with hers occurred, a sudden sensation swept over our faces, causing her to move back a bit. Neither she could meet my gaze nor could I.

She shyly turned her face away, and I, too, feeling hesitant, appeared lost as if everything had just been discovered and a little more was yet to be found. Then Shehnaz came up on the roof and said, "That's why I wasn't coming down. Now look." She turned her face upwards, sulking, and I, feeling hesitant, seemed as if my eyes were trying to connect with hers, my lips were talking to hers, and holding both her hands in mine, they too were conversing with each other. After a while, Rose asked Shehnaz, "What's the matter?

Tell me, why aren't you speaking?" After she asked this, I was hesitantly looking at Rose and she was looking hesitantly at me. Neither of us had an answer to this question. Meanwhile, Shehnaz kept asking, and we kept hesitating.

After some time, Rose said, "(to Shehnaz) We're feeling a bit strange, that's why we're here to sleep." (to Rose) "Okay, fine. Until we finish talking, you guys go." The expression on Rose's face changed so much that it seemed she didn't want to leave us alone on the roof. After Shehnaz said this, we both held hands and sat straight and Shehnaz sat next to us. Then she asked, "Hey, tell me, why aren't you saying anything? Okay, you tell me what happened first?" After asking this, Rose hesitantly looked at me and then hesitantly looked towards Shehnaz. While Shehnaz kept asking, we kept hesitating.

A little later, Shehnaz said, "(to Rose) We're feeling a bit strange, that's why we're here to sleep." (to Rose) "Okay, fine. Until we finish talking, you guys go." After this, Shehnaz held our hands and led us straight to the gate and sat down next to us.

Then she said, "Let's talk about what happened after we leave them downstairs." After Shehnaz took us downstairs to the hostel gate and asked me, "Do you like Shehnaz?" I said, "If I like many girls in the hostel, will you arrange for me to talk to all of them?"

Rose said, "If we start making noise here, you know what will happen?" Kushagra was listening to all these things standing at the gate with us, and after hearing Rose's statement about making noise, he bowed his head in front of Rose with folded hands and said, "No Devi Ji, there's no need to make noise.

This is a straightforward person who has never been able to understand that he should talk to girls. I apologize on his behalf." Upon hearing Kushagra say this, Rose turned towards me and said, "Go, take this drunkard upstairs. Looks like he's overdosed today." Kushagra, saying this to Rose, gave me another affectionate taunt and said to me, "Come on, Dev Purush, let's go upstairs to your room and you are completely intoxicated. You have freed all the kids of the hostel from addiction."

After saying this, Rose left for her room feeling embarrassed and Kushagra also wanted to talk to me before going to sleep, but on Rose's insistence, he went to sleep, and I... After two hours of sleep, as per the routine, when we reached class, we felt that our way of studying was going to be disrupted again, and that's exactly what happened. Most of the time, we slept or whispered to the teacher.

When we stepped out of class two or three times, we saw that Shehnaz and Kushagra were in the same state as us.

But Rose studied, wrote, and understood with us every time. Seeing Rose like this every time, I, too, silently thought that maybe Kushagra isn't wrong —there's something different.

In this girl, before whom we all are useless. After the class ended, we all reached the hostel and everyone slept. On waking up in the evening, the same thoughts began to swirl in the mind again, whether she will come to meet me on the rooftop every day after what happened yesterday or not?

When I told Kushagra about this problem, he suggested an idea. According to the suggestion, I had to ask Shahnaaz to come to the rooftop after dinner. As per the plan, Shahnaaz arrived around 10:00 PM.

Even after spending a whole hour on Shahnaaz's rooftop, when she didn't come to the rooftop the next day, I also started feeling restless and understood that I didn't like the events of last night. Even after two hours passed and she didn't come to the rooftop, I went to the girls' hostel rooftop with Shahnaaz's help. Where we sat yesterday, I sat there again and had Shahnaaz by my side. Some girls knew about my daily visits to the rooftop.

Vandana had already seen me coming towards the rooftop. Shahnaaz kept discussing the same topic with me while sitting there, how long I had been in love with her. But my mind was only focused on Shahnaaz's daily absence on the rooftop.

I had asked Shahnaaz several times to call her upstairs, but she always made excuses about being unwell and changed the topic - finally, I said to Shahnaaz,

"Shahnaaz, if you don't mind, can you sit here with me for the next 2 or 3 hours?" And then I also told Shahnaaz that I will definitely tell you the reason for my sitting alone on the rooftop tomorrow.

Hearing my words, Shahnaaz went downstairs. I sat alone on the rooftop for half an hour, and then half an hour later, she came to the rooftop again and sat far away from me. I got up and went to her and sat beside her. Well, we weren't even looking at each other from here. I kept asking her why she didn't come to the rooftop for a long time, and she remained silent, without saying anything.

When she didn't respond to me for the next half an hour, I held her hand in mine and asked her why she didn't come to the rooftop. In response to my question, she said to me, "Every day - can we claim our rights on you or can we own you? Think and give an answer."

I said, "Yes, of course, why not?" (I said with joy in my heart) She said, "Sure, right?" I said, "Yes, why not! If we don't accept each other from within, we wouldn't sit here. Tell me, what do I need to say, understanding each other? I was happy inside because I knew that the three-letter word of love is coming from the front.

And then, I eagerly awaited those words. Rose asked me to close my eyes and told me that she won't be able to do what she wants to with my eyes open.

Hearing all this, I also became excited and started closing my eyes. As I closed my eyes, I felt uncomfortable waiting, suddenly I felt a slap on my cheek. I opened my eyes and saw that there was no one around, only Rose was sitting in front. Before I could ask her the reason for this, she started crying.

When I tried to wipe her tears and make her quiet, I realized that she had a high fever. One thing I forgot to tell you is that she had a lot of trust in vows, so after making many promises and trying to silence her, when I wanted to know the reason for the slap by asking Shahnaaz, she started telling all about Shahnaaz and me, and then asked me, "Rose - today if we had a fever, why did you talk to Shahnaaz on the rooftop for hours?" And then you also came to meet her here."

"Can you talk to Shahnaaz for us?" Yes, I will try to talk to her only when I feel like it. :- No-no, we're not. Don't you talk to her anymore. Now we've become such good friends that you shouldn't even think of talking to her. Okay, I won't talk to Shahnaaz for you. I promise. I'll do one more thing for you right now.

"What?" I'll tell you all about it. And extend your hand and place it on my head. She placed her hand on my head. Now you swear to me, you won't do anything for the next 5 minutes, you'll just say it.

Then she kept quiet and didn't say anything. While I kept staring at her, she kept looking at me curiously, wondering what 'Saj' was going to say. I grabbed Rose's wrist with my right hand and reached out with my left hand towards her head, pulling her closer, I came so close to her that her hair touched mine, her eyes met mine, her face touched mine, and her lips touched mine. After a few seconds of staying like this, I leaned back again.

The text translates to:

"Shahnaz was surprised, looking at me with wide eyes, and to some extent, Rose too, and I smiled while saying two such lines to her as I entered my hostel, which might still be echoing in her ears even after I left. When I was whispering these lines to Shahnaz, I stepped back. Then I said to Rose - 'Don't call me a friend next time, because we are not friends anymore.

Love you - love you and you love me - me - me.' How do I explain to you all about my journey of love, which lasted only seven and a half days? The price of these seven and a half days was so high that it became a reason for me to come and live in the world of stars. In these seven and a half days, I learned three types of love and traversed the paths of all three types of love.

I have shared these three types of love with you

by giving them the form of three moments. And this is the first moment of our agreement. You must have heard that in an agreement, there is a big disagreement, and such an agreement is also not fun, in which there is no disagreement. So let's embark on this disagreement journey.

After entering the girls' hostel, I was heading towards the roof, and Rose was still helping me to reach the roof, but one thing was spinning in my mind repeatedly. Kushagra had told me that brother, you are going to the girls' hostel, but if these two sisters make any move, or if they harm you in any way (catch you in the girls' hostel), then hug your friend for the last time. Because after that, only your God will save you. In response to Kushagra's words, I said – 'If these girls don't let me go, today we are going to become their gods.

'Just a while later, I reached the roof. Rose had also reached there along with me. I went towards one corner of the roof and sat down. Rose came and sat next to me. Rose said - Aren't you afraid? I said - First tell me how did you know about the key to the girls' hostel? Rose - Oh, she was standing by the window in the evening, so I heard Saurav's voice. He was saying to Vandana, why are these Kushagra and his friend lurking around the watchman's cabin? Just by that, I figured out that because of your capability, I trust you completely in these matters. Without saying what's in your mind, how can you come back? - Well, that's fine.

I didn't understand your new way of talking, speaking in 'tu-tu' manner. Meaning, this 'tu' word is being used because I was sitting in the girls' hostel. Imagine, you will be called 'tum' more than me when you are in front of others. - Oh no! When you are in front of everyone, we should show respect.

That's why we call you 'tum' in front of everyone, and likewise, we will speak. - That's right. The person in front calls himself 'tu' and me 'tum'.

Okay, tell me one thing, will anyone doubt that you stayed here all night? - We have a different kind of bond in Galser, and maybe you have enough respect in Galser. - Why, I haven't even saved anyone's honor (I said). - No, you didn't save the honor, but many girls say that whenever there was an argument between girls and boys, you would come and take the girl away.

Yes, maybe, but I didn't pay attention. They were both still talking when Shahnaz arrived on the roof. - Are you both sitting here on the roof? By the way, you are sitting in the right place, don't look from anywhere else, even if someone comes on the roof, don't look.

By the way, you shouldn't be too scared because some girls are like that if someone goes, they might find you hiding in their bed. - What you are saying is true, brother. If anything happens, the friend won't survive either. If you kick me out, then I'll put a lock on the ground floor with Kushagra's help. - Yes, but how will you tell Kushagra?

I gestured to Kushagra from the roof, asking if the girls had complained, what should I do now? Kushagra started speaking from below - "No, brother, don't kick me. The friend won't survive even a day there. Please don't kick me, otherwise, with this mafia, I'll have to drink hot water for the rest of my life in jail." I gestured to Kushagra again and explained the whole thing again, and Kushagra locked the door and went back to the watchman. And I came down to them and sat down. Rose - So Dadda will play all night for this bribe.

I said - No, don't leave anything. Shahnaz - Do you like any girl in the hostel? I said looking at Shahnaz's face - "Yes, you." Shahnaz - Who, me or

Saj? I said - You, because Saj and I are enemies, right, we can't be one. Fate has written this in its own way, and that too with ink. Rose - (said to Shahnaz) If she doesn't like you, will you like her? I said - (to Rose) Someone told me that I don't like Shahnaz. Rose - Shahnaz must have already said yes to you. There won't be any status like that, will there be? You'll have to propose to it first. Or else confirm it, whether you love it or not, after proposing it. Shahnaz - (said to me) Saj is right, now I haven't confirmed anything."

Suddenly, Rose said to Shahnaaz, "Go down and check once, there shouldn't be any problem." Shahnaaz got up and went down, and my mind was spinning here. I kept thinking, why did she send Shahnaaz down? And is it because I don't want to talk to Shahnaaz? With these thoughts in mind, when I looked at Rose again, she looked strange.

I felt like she wanted to say something to me but hesitated. Then I asked myself, does Rose like me? And if my mind didn't find the answer to this question, I asked myself another question, whom do I like more, Rose or Shahnaaz? When I closed my eyes to find the answer to this question, I found only one answer: "Rose, every day." Then I looked at Rose again and held both her hands from wrists and palms. She didn't say anything and seemed a bit nervous. Then I asked Rose for permission. "Can I lean on your shoulder?" She still didn't say anything and lowered her eyes, tilting her face slightly.

As I moved closer to put my head on her shoulder, she didn't move her head towards me, but her face turned slightly as if my eyes were talking to her tilted eyes, my lips were talking to her cheeks, and my hands holding hers were also communicating with each other. Even then, when she seemed hesitant to say anything, I also hesitated, and while agreeing, I tried to bring our eyes closer. When the proximity increased, it felt like my eyelashes were touching hers, and when the tips of our eyelashes touched, a sudden excitement spread across our faces, causing her to look away after a few moments. Neither she nor I could meet each other's gaze.

She shyly turned her face away, and I too seemed lost, as if I had just found everything and was now trying to gain a little more, when Shahnaaz suddenly appeared on the roof and said, "That's why I wasn't going down. Now look." Maharani ji was looking there, sitting with her face down, and these gentlemen here seemed restless without her. "Come on, let's go straight down now and settle whatever argument you two had," Shahnaaz said, holding both of our hands and sitting us down.

Then she asked, "Tell me, why aren't you speaking? Alright, tell me what happened first? After asking this, while looking at Rose with tearful eyes, I was looking at Shahnaaz and she was looking at me hesitantly. Neither of us had an answer to this question. Shahnaaz kept asking while we remained silent.

A little later, Rose and Shahnaaz said, "We're feeling a bit weird, so we're going to bed. Let's go." Rose said, "Okay, you guys go, we'll talk later," her expression changed so much that it seemed like she didn't want to leave me alone on the roof. After Shahnaaz said this, Rose went to the other corner of the roof, saying, "We'll spend some time on the roof for a while, maybe feel better."

While looking at Rose, Shahnaaz said, "Alright, let's go for a walk, but don't pay attention to us, because now love and confession talks are about to begin here." (Shahnaaz had leaned her head on my shoulder while saying this) At that moment, I could understand either Rose's condition or Rose's. Rose's head was on my shoulder, and I was constantly looking at Rose.

Rose's eyes were fixed on my shoulder. I could understand Rose's discomfort at that moment, so I got up and signalled to open the lock. Then I went to Rose and asked her to come down, she gestured towards Shahnaaz with her eyes, as if taunting me to go and take her.

After this gesture, I approached Shahnaaz and she moved away from me saying, "We'll leave it downstairs and come back to tell you what happened." Rose brought me downstairs to the hostel gate and asked me, "Do you like Shahnaaz? If I like many girls in the hostel, will you get me engaged to all of them?" After this, Rose and I were listening to everything standing at the gate, and when Rose heard the noise, she bowed her head and apologised to me by holding my hand and said, "No, Goddess, you don't need to make noise. This is an outspoken person who has not yet understood that he should be courteous to girls. I apologize on his behalf."

On hearing Kushagra's words, I turned back and replied, "Every day: Go, take this addict upstairs. It seems like he's overdosed today." Kushagra, while giving another taunt every day, said to me, "Let's go, Dev, let's go upstairs to your room, and you are completely intoxicated. You have freed all the kids in the hostel from addiction." Hearing this taunt every day, I went up to my room in anger, and he to his.

Kushagra wanted to talk to me before sleeping, but upon my insistence to talk in the morning, he went to sleep and I went to mine. After two hours of sleep, when we reached the class according to our timetable, we felt that our way of studying was going to be disrupted again, and it did. Most of the time, we slept through the classes, ignoring the teacher.

During class, two or three times when we went out of our class, we saw that Shahnaaz and Kushagra were also in the same state as us. But Rose met us every day, teaching, writing, and understanding us. Seeing this every day, I too silently admitted to myself that Kushagra wasn't wrong. There's something different about this girl in front of whom we all are useless.

After the class ended, we all returned to the hostel and everyone had a good night's sleep. In the evening, as I woke up, the same thoughts started swirling in my mind again - will Rose come to meet me on the roof tomorrow or not? When I told Kushagra about this problem, he suggested something.

According to his suggestion, I had to ask Shahnaaz to come to the roof after dinner. Following the plan, Shahnaaz came to the roof around 10:00 at night. Even after an hour of being on Shahnaaz's roof, when Rose didn't come, I also started feeling anxious and understood that Rose didn't like what happened last night. Even after two hours had passed, when Rose didn't come to the roof, I sought Shahnaaz's help and went to the roof of Girls Hostel.

I sat where we had sat yesterday, and Shahnaaz was beside me. Some girls knew about my daily visits to the roof. Vandana had also seen me coming to the roof. Shahnaaz kept talking to me about when I had started loving her. But my attention was focused on Rose's absence and I wasn't interested in talking about it with Shahnaaz.

I had asked Shahnaaz many times to call Rose upstairs, but she always diverted the topic by saying that Rose was not feeling well. Finally, I told Shahnaaz firmly that if she didn't mind, I could sit here for 2 or 3 more hours. And then I told her that tomorrow night I would tell her the reason for my sitting alone on the roof. After hearing me, Shahnaaz went downstairs. I sat alone on the roof for half an hour, waiting for Rose to come.

Then after half an hour, when se came to the roof, she sat far away from me. I got up and went to her and sat beside her. It was good that we weren't visible to anyone from here.

For a long time, I kept asking her why she didn't come to the roof, and she kept sitting silently, without saying anything. When she didn't answer me for the next half an hour, I held her hand and asked her why she didn't come to the roof. In response to my question, she said to me: "Can we claim our rights on you, or do you claim your own? Think and answer. Yes, why not? If we don't accept ourselves from within, then we wouldn't sit here. Tell me, what is there to tell, understand yourself? I was secretly happy because I knew that the three magical words of love were about to come out.

And then, eagerly waiting for those words, I started looking at her. Rose asked me to close my eyes and told me that what she wanted to do, she wouldn't be able to do it with my eyes open. Hearing all this, I became excited and started closing my eyes.

While closing my eyes, I was feeling uneasy in anticipation, as suddenly I felt a slap on my cheek. When I opened my eyes to see, there was no one around, just Rose sitting in front of me. Before I could ask her the reason for this, she started crying. When I wiped her tears and tried to calm her down, I felt that she had a high fever. I forgot to tell you one thing, I trusted her a lot, so I tried to silence her by swearing many times and then tried to find out the reason for the slap by swearing and asking Vandana and me, but she started all our conversations and then asked me why I had come to the roof to meet Shahnaaz for hours. When I asked her the reason for my question, she started crying.

When I wiped her tears and tried to silence her by swearing many times, I felt that she had a high fever. When I wiped her tears and tried to silence her, I felt that she had a high fever. Before I could ask her the reason for the slap, she started crying.

When I wiped her tears and tried to silence her, I felt that she had a high fever. Before I could ask her the reason for the slap, she started crying. When I wiped her tears and tried to silence her, I felt that she had a high fever. When I asked her the reason for my question, she started crying. When I wiped her tears and tried to silence her, I felt that she had a high fever.

Before I could ask her the reason for the slap, she started crying. When I wiped her tears and tried to silence her, I felt that she had a high fever. When I asked her the reason for my question, she started crying. When I wiped her tears and tried to silence her, I felt that she had a high fever.

Before I could ask her the reason for the slap, she started crying. When I wiped her tears and tried to silence her, I felt that she had a high fever. When I asked her the reason for my question, she started crying. When I wiped her tears and tried to silence her, I felt that she had a high fever. Before I could ask her the reason for the slap, she started crying. When I wiped her tears and tried to silence her, I felt that she had a high fever.

When I asked her the reason for my question, she started crying. When I wiped her tears and tried to silence her, I felt that she had a high fever.

Before I could ask her the reason for the slap, she

started crying. When I wiped her tears and tried to silence her, I felt that she had a high fever.

When I asked her the reason for my question, she started crying. When I wiped her tears and tried to silence her, I felt that she had a high fever. Before I could ask her the reason for the slap, she started crying.

When I wiped her tears and tried to silence her, I felt that she had a high fever. When I asked her the reason for my question, she started crying.

When I wiped her tears and tried to silence her, I felt that she had a high fever.

I: Okay, fine. I won't talk to Shahnaaz ever again. I promise. Yes, I'll do one more thing for you right now.

Rose: What?

I: I'll tell you everything. And bring your hand and place it on my head.

Rose placed her hand on my head.

I: Now, it's your turn. For the next 5 minutes, you won't do anything or say anything.

She remained silent, eagerly waiting for me to speak. When I had taken this oath from Rose, Shahnaaz had come to the rooftop and sat near us. Shahnaaz was continuously looking at us curiously, wondering what Saaj was about to say.

I grabbed Rose's wrist with my right hand and brought my left hand towards her head, holding her for a while like this, coming so close to her, her hair intertwined with mine, her eyes meeting mine, her face so close to mine, and her lips brushing against mine.

After a few seconds in this position, I moved back. Shahnaaz was astonished, staring at me, and Rose also, smiling, silently following me. After saying two such lines, I went back to my hostel, which even after I left, must have been echoing in her ears.

When Rose was moving back by glancing at me after unlocking her lips from mine, I said to Rose:

Next time, don't call me a friend, because we're not friends anymore. Love you - love you and you love me - me- me - 'Roj-Roj-Everyday'. How do I tell you all that my journey of love lasted only seven and a half days? The value of these seven and a half days was so much that it became the reason for this journey I came to live in the world of stars.

In these seven and a half days, I learned three types of love and passed through the paths of all three types of love. I have shared with you these three types of love by giving them the form of three moments. And this is the first moment of our agreement.

You must have heard that there is a big argument in agreement, and such an agreement is also not fun in which there is no argument. After entering the Girls Hostel, I was going towards the roof, and Rose was helping me to reach the roof, but a thing was repeatedly wandering in my mind.

Kushagra had told me that brother, you are going to Girls Hostel, but if these two sisters make any move, or if they change you in any way (by catching you in the Girls Hostel), then hug your friend for the last time. Because later, only your God is the owner. In response to Kushagra's words, I said - "If these girls don't take action, then today we are going to become their gods".

Just a little later, I had reached the roof. Rose had also arrived there with me. I went towards the other side of the roof and sat down. Rose also came and sat beside me. Rose - Aren't you afraid?

I - First tell me how did you know about the key thing, Rose? Rose - Oh, she was standing at the window in the evening, so I heard Saurav's voice. He was telling Vandana that why are these two, Kushagra and his friend, looking for the watchman's quarters?

Just from that, I understood because I have full confidence in your ability in such matters. Without influencing your mind, how can you come back. I - Okay, everything is fine. I didn't understand this new way of talking with you.

I mean, why is the word 'you' being used, because I am sitting in Girls Hostel. Just imagine, I will also be called 'you' more than 'you' then. Rose - Oh no! When you are in front of everyone, we should respect you. That's why we call you 'you' in front of everyone, and we will say the same. I - That's right. The person in front calls himself 'I' and me 'you'. Okay, tell me, won't anyone doubt where you were when you stayed here all night?

Rose - We have a different kind of bond in Girls and maybe you won't have it, that girls respect you a lot in Girls. I - Why, I didn't even save anyone's respect (I said). No, respect is not saved, but many girls say that when there was a debate with a boy, you would take him away. Maybe, but I didn't pay attention. They were just talking when Shahnaaz came to the roof.

Are both of you sitting here? By the way, you are sitting in the right place, leave it from somewhere else, don't even see the roof, even if someone comes to the roof.

Otherwise, don't be afraid because some girls are like this, if someone goes for a chance, they can find you in their bed. - What you're saying is sure that I won't get caught, because if that happens, I'll get the lock of Kushagra's room downstairs. - Yes, it's for sure, but how will you tell Kushagra ?

"I lifted two or three bricks from the roof and hit the guard with a rod near the boys' hostel. As Kushagra came there, I signaled to him to lock up and went back to the guard. And I sat down after coming back to both of them. - So, this man will play cards all night for a bribe. No, don't let it go,

Kush.

The hostel girls hostel will not even leave a bone behind. Please don't let it go, brother, otherwise, I will have to drink jail water with this guy." I gestured to Kushagra again and explained the whole thing to him again, Kushagra locked it up and went back to the guy. And I came and sat between the two.

- So this guy will complain all night in exchange for a bribe. No, Kush, don't leave it. :- Do you like any girl in the hostel? Looking at Shahnaaz, I said - you." Shahnaaz: - To whom, me or Saj? Me: - To you, because Saj and I are enemies, right, we can't be one at all - fate has written this in its destiny, without erasing it with ink.

Every day: - (said to Shahnaaz) If she doesn't like you, will you like her? Me: - (from Rose) Who told you that I don't like Shahnaaz?

Every day: - (said to Shahnaaz) Shahnaaz, your already will be yes from the beginning. Won't there be such a status, will you have to propose it first? Or then consider it after confirming it, whether you love it or not, after proposing it. Shahnaaz: - (said to me) This thing Saj is saying correctly, I don't have any confirmation yet. Yes, if you propose, then maybe I can.

Then suddenly Rose said to Shahnaaz- "Shahnaz, go down and see once, there is no problem." Shahnaz got up and went down and my mind was spinning here. I kept thinking the same thing, why is she going round and round to talk to Shahnaaz? And has she sent Shahnaz down so that I don't talk to Shahnaz?

I kept thinking, when I looked at Rose again, she was weird. Seeing her, I felt that she might want to say something to me and hesitate. Here again I asked myself a question, does Rose like me?

And if I don't find the answer to this question by my heart, then I asked myself another question, whom do I like more, Rose or Shahnaz? When I closed my eyes to know the answer to this question, I found only one answer, 'Roj-Roj-every day'. I looked at Rose again and held her hands with both my hands and hands. She didn't say anything and was slightly shocked. Again, I asked Rose for permission. Can I keep my head on your head? She didn't say anything again and kept looking down and bowed her head.

And as I tried to bring my face closer by moving forward, she didn't touch my head, but turned her face in a way as if my eyes were talking to her half-closed eyes, my lips were talking to her cheeks, and my hands in her hands were also talking to each other.

But even then when she didn't say anything shyly, I also hesitated and with agreement, I reached my eyes from her eyes with my eyes and wanted to go a little closer, so close-ups increased so much, as if my both eyelashes were touching her both eyelashes, somewhere in her eyes She was trying to lose herself, her lips were talking to my cheeks, and when my eyelashes touched her eyelashes, then an excited excitement happened on our faces, as if after a few moments she turned back. Neither was she able to see me nor was I able to.

She shyly turned her face back and I was also lost as if I had just found everything and just a little more effort was needed, then Shahnaz went up on the roof and said - Look, that's why I was not going down.

Now see, that queen is sitting there, sitting with her mouth open, and these gentlemen are not able to live without fighting. Come on, now both of you straighten up and after arguing with each other about this matter, you both now. After this, Shahnaz holds both of our hands and sits straight with us and asks Rose again- Tell me, why aren't you telling?

Okay Saj, you tell me first, what happened to you? After asking this question, I was shocked and was looking towards Rose and she was looking at me in surprise. None of us had an answer to this question."

Here's the translation of the text into English:

"Here, Shahnaz kept asking, and we agreed. After a while, Rose and Shahnaz said - Rose: (to Shahnaz) We're feeling a bit strange, so we're going to sleep. Shahnaz: (to Rose) Okay, as long as I and he talk, you go.

The expression on Rose's face changed so much that it seemed she didn't want to leave me and Shahnaz alone on the roof.

Upon hearing Shahnaz's words, Rose went to the other corner of the roof - Rose: Let's spend some time on the roof for a while, maybe it'll feel good. Shahnaz: (looking at Rose and speaking to Rose)

Okay, let's go, but listen, don't pay attention to us here, because now things are going to start about love and confession.

(Shahnaz said this to Rose and put her head on my shoulder) At that time, I could understand Rose's condition well, or Rose. Shahnaz had her head on my shoulder, and I kept looking at Rose continuously. Rose's gaze was fixed on my shoulder. Rose's condition at that time, I could understand well, or Rose.

When Shahnaz said this, Rose went to Kushagra and gestured to lock and open the door. Then I went to Rose and told her to let me down, she gestured to Shahnaz with her eyes, as if saying, take her down, leave her here. After this gesture, I had taken a few steps towards Shahnaz, but Rose's voice came from behind - Rose: Shahnaz, let's take this druggie upstairs, seems like he's overdosed today.

Then, teasing Rose once again, I said to her - Let's go, gentlemen, let's go upstairs to our room, and you, you're completely intoxicated. You've freed all the kids from the hostel's intoxication. With this tease from Rose, she went to her room and we to ours. Kushagra wanted to talk to me before sleeping, but upon hearing Rose's words, he went to sleep, and I.

After sleeping for a few hours, when we reached class according to the schedule, we felt that our way of studying was going to be disorganized again, and that's what happened. Most of the time, we slept after sneaking from the teacher.

When we went out of class two or three times, we saw that Shahnaz and Kushagra were also in the same state as us. But Rose, every time she saw us, she studied, wrote, and understood with us.

Seeing Rose like this every time, I too silently kept saying to myself that Kushagra is not wrong - there's something different about this girl, in front of whom we're all worthless. After the class ended, we all reached the hostel and everyone slept. In the evening, when I woke up, the same thoughts started spinning in my mind - will Rose come to the roof to meet me tomorrow or not?

I told Kushagra about this problem, so he suggested something. According to the plan, I was supposed to ask Shahnaaz to come to the roof after dinner. As per the plan, Shahnaaz came to the roof around 10:00 at night. Even after spending a whole hour on Shahnaaz's roof, when Rose didn't come to the roof, I also became mentally restless and understood that Rose didn't like the antics of last night. Even after two hours passed, when Rose didn't come to the roof, I went to the roof of the girls' hostel with Shahnaaz's help. Where we had sat yesterday, I sat there again and Shahnaaz came to sit beside me.

Some girls knew about my daily visit to the roof. Vandana had also seen me coming towards the roof. Shahnaaz kept talking to me about how long I had loved her. But my attention was fixed on Rose, not Shahnaaz.

I asked Shahnaaz several times to call her upstairs, but she kept changing the topic by saying that Rose was unwell. Finally, I finally said to Shahnaaz - 'Shahnaaz, if you don't mind, can I sit on your roof for the next 2 or 3 hours?' And then I also told Shahnaaz that I would tell her the reason for sitting on the roof tomorrow. Hearing my words, Shahnaaz went down. I sat on the roof alone for half an hour and then Rose came to the roof and sat far away from me, avoiding each other. I got up and went to her and sat down beside her.

Well, it was good that even from here we weren't showing ourselves to anyone. For a long time, I kept asking her why she didn't come to the roof, and she kept sitting silently, without saying anything.

When she didn't give me an answer even after the next half hour, I held her hand in mine and asked her why she didn't come to the roof.

Hearing my question, she said to me - 'Can we claim our right over you, or do you own it? Think carefully and answer. Yes, why not? Absolutely! If we didn't believe in our uniqueness from within, we wouldn't sit here.

Tell me what you want to tell, understanding your own.' I was secretly happy because I knew that in front of her, the word 'love' and 'confession' were about to come. And then I eagerly looked at her waiting for those words. Rose told me to close my eyes and told me that what she wanted to do, she wouldn't be able to do with my eyes wide open.

Here's the translation of the text into English:

"After hearing all this, I felt relieved and closed my eyes in anticipation. As I closed my eyes, I felt a sudden slap on my cheek. When I opened my eyes, there was no one around, only Rose sitting in front of me. Before I could ask her about it, she started crying. When I tried to wipe away her tears and calm her down, I realized that she had a high fever.

I forgot to tell you one thing, I had a lot of faith in her oaths, so I tried to get her to be quiet by making her swear, wanting to know the reason for the slap. Then she asked me: "Today, if we had a fever, why did you spend hours talking to Shahnaaz on the roof after calling her? And then you came here to meet her." Do you want to talk to Shahnaaz for us?

Me: Yes, I will try to talk to her only when necessary. Rose: No, no, we don't want that. Don't talk to her at all. Now we have become such good friends that you don't need to listen to her. Now we have become such good friends that you don't need to listen to her.

Me: Okay, I won't talk to Shahnaaz for you. I promise. Yes, I'll do one more thing for you right now. Rose: "What?" Me: I'll tell you everything. And I reached out my hand and placed it on her head. Rose put her hand on my head. Me: Now you have my oath, for the next 5 minutes, you won't do anything or say anything.

Then she remained silent, without saying anything, waiting for me to say something. Meanwhile, Shahnaaz came to the roof and sat next to us. Shahnaaz was looking surprised, blinking her eyes, and to some extent, Rose was also wondering what 'Saj' was about to say.

I reached out with my right hand and grabbed Rose's wrist, and with my left hand, I leaned towards her, holding her for a while like this, getting so close to her, her hair mingled with mine, her eyes with mine, her face with mine, and her lips with mine. After a few seconds of staying like this, I backed off. Shahnaaz was astonished, blinking her eyes, and Rose was also smiling.

Finally, I said two lines to Rose and went to my hostel, which must have echoed in her ears even after I left. When Rose was sweeping aside, I said to her, 'Next time don't call me a friend.

Because we are no longer friends, we are I Love You - I Love You and You Love Me - Me - Me -'Roj-Roj-Everyday'. How can I tell you all that my journey of love lasted only for seven and a half days? The price of these seven and a half days was so high that it became a reason, that I came to stay in the world of stars. In these seven and a half days, I learned three types of love and passed through the paths of all three types of love.

I have shared with you the form of all three types of love in three moments. And this is the first moment of our confession. You must have heard that in confession, there is a big argument, and such a confession is not fun in which there is no argument.

After entering the girls' hostel, I was going

towards the roof and Rose was also helping me to reach there, but a thought was revolving in my mind repeatedly because of Kushagra's words.

Kushagra had told me that brother, you are going to the girls' hostel, but if these two sisters play any tricks, or if you see any change in them (catch them in the girls' hostel), then hug them tightly for the last time. Because after that, your God is alone. In response to Kushagra's words, I said - "If these girls didn't take the step, then today we are going to become their God." Shortly after, I reached the roof. Rose had also reached there with me. I went towards the other side of the roof and sat down. Rose also came and sat next to me.

- Aren't you afraid? First tell me how did you come to know about the key of the hostel's duplicate lock?

- Oh, when Vandana was standing at the window in the evening, I heard Saurav's voice. He was saying to Vandana, why are these two sisters looking so suspicious? I just understood from this that you have complete faith in your capabilities. How can you come back without expressing your mind?"

Certainly! Here is the translation of the text into English:

"I - Okay, everything is fine, but I didn't understand your new way of talking with 'tu-tu.' I mean, why is the word 'tu' being used because I am sitting in Girls Hostel. Think about it, I won't even be addressed with 'tum' much.

Daily - Oh no! When you are in front of everyone, we should give respect. That's why we address you as 'tum' in front of everyone, and you should do the same. Me - That's right. The person in front calls themselves 'hum' and me 'tu.' Okay, tell me one thing, won't anyone have doubts about where you were when you stayed here all night?

Daily - We have a different bond in Girls and maybe you don't have that. Maybe you have enough respect in Girls. Me - Why, I haven't even saved anyone's respect (I said). Daily - No, you haven't saved respect, but many girls say that many times when the argument of girls happened with a boy, you dragged the boy there. Me - Yes, maybe, but I didn't pay attention. We were still talking when Shahnaaz came upstairs. Shahnaaz - Are you both sitting here? By the way, you are sitting in the right place, leave it, no matter where you are, don't look up. By the way, don't be too scared because some girls are like if anyone goes to their room, they may find you in their bed. Me - Is it true that Dadda will pay you all night as a bribe? No, don't tease him. Even Haddi won't be spared if teased from there. Brother, please don't tease, otherwise, I'll have to drink jail water with this ghost." I gestured again to explain the whole thing to Dadda, and he walked back to the Boys' Hostel. And I came back and sat down with both of them.

"So Dadda will pay him all night as a bribe. No, don't leave anything. :-(You like a girl in the hostel?" Shahnaaz turns her face and asks. "To whom? Me, you, or Saj?" "You, because Saj and I are enemies, right, we can't be one." Fate has written in its own way, not to mention ignoring. If she doesn't like you, who will you like? Rose asked, "No, someone must have said to you that I don't like Shahnaaz."

Shahnaaz said, "Shahnaaz will already say yes to you." Will there be such a status that you have to propose it first? Or confirm it again whether you love it or not after proposing. "Shahnaaz is saying the right thing," she said, "I don't have any confirmation now." Suddenly Rose said, "Shahnaaz, come downstairs and see, there is no problem." Shahnaaz got up and went downstairs, and my mind was spinning here. I was constantly thinking, why did she send Shahnaaz down?

Whether I should talk to Shahnaaz or not. I kept thinking, and when I looked at Rose, she was strange. I held both her hands and wrists and looked at them, as if my eyes were talking to her squinted eyes, my lips were talking to her cheeks, and my hands were talking to hers, and when our eyes met, a moment of excitement happened, as if she had looked away after a few moments. Neither she could meet my eyes nor I hers.

Shyly, she turned her face away and I too was shy as if I had found everything and just wanted a little more, then Shahnaaz went up to the roof and said, "That's why I wasn't going downstairs.

Now see, the queen is sulking, sitting there, and these gentlemen, without them, can't get peace. Come on, both of you go straight and now you two quarrel over this matter. After this, Shahnaaz grabbed both of our hands and made us sit down and sat down next to us. Then she asked again, "Why aren't you telling me, tell me why?" Okay, Saj, you tell me first, what happened? After asking this question, when Rose looked at me with hesitant eyes, I kept looking at Rose, and she was looking at me hesitantly.

We kept agreeing with each other, while Shahnaaz kept asking some questions and we kept agreeing. After a while, Rose said to Shahnaaz, "We are feeling a little strange, so we are staying here to sleep." Shahnaaz said to Rose, "Okay, when we talk more, you go." Rose's facial expressions changed so much after this dispute, as if she didn't want to leave me alone on the roof."

Upon hearing Shahnaz's words, I turned towards the other corner of the rooftop.

Shahnaz: (looking towards the daily, she said) "Alright, let's stroll on the rooftop for a while. Maybe it'll feel good."

Me: (looking towards the daily) "Okay, let's stroll, but listen, don't pay attention to me because now, some talks about love and acceptance are about to start here." (Shahnaz said this to me, laying her head on my shoulder) At that moment, I could understand either my or Rose's condition.

Shahnaz's head was on my shoulder, and I kept watching Rose continuously. Rose's gaze was fixed on my shoulder. At that time, I could understand Rose's discomfort very well, so I stood up and gestured towards the gate to open it. Then I went to Rose and asked her to come down, she gestured towards Shahnaz with her eyes, as if saying, "Take her away." After her gesture, I took a few steps towards Shahnaz. Just as I was about to reach her, Rose's voice came from behind - Rose: "Shahnaz, let's take this down to the bottom and tell what happened. Rose took me down to the gate of the girls' hostel and asked me - Rose: "Do you like Shahnaz?" Me: "If I liked many girls from the hostel, would you arrange a talk for me with all of them?" Rose: "If we start making noise here, who knows what will happen?"

Kushagra was standing with us at the gate, listening to all these things, and when Rose started making noise, he joined Rose, clasped his hands, bowed his head, gave a loving gesture to Rose, and said, "No, madam, there's no need for you to make noise.

This is an outspoken person, and he still hasn't learned that he should talk to girls." From his side, I apologize to you." After Kushagra said this, Rose turned to me and said - "Go, take this addict upstairs, it seems like she's overdosed today." Giving another taunt to Rose, she said to me - "Let's go, gentleman, let's go upstairs to our rooms, and you are completely intoxicated."

You have made all the kids of the hostel drug-free." After hearing this taunt from Rose, I went to my room, and Kushagra wanted to talk to me before sleeping, but on my saying, he went to sleep there, and I went to sleep. When we reached the class according to the timetable the next day, we felt that our way of studying is going to be disrupted again, and it happened. Most of the time, we slept hiding from the teacher.

When we went out of our class two or three times in between the classes, we saw that Shahnaz and Kushagra were in the same condition as us. But Rose met us, taught us, and understood us every time.

Seeing Rose like this every time, I also felt relieved and quietly said to myself - "Kushagra is not wrong - there is something different in this girl, before which we all are useless." After the class ended, we all reached the hostel and everyone slept. When I woke up in the evening, the thought started swirling in my mind again - will Rose come to meet me on the rooftop after what happened yesterday or not?

When I told Kushagra about this problem,

he suggested something. According to the suggestion, I had to tell Shahnaz to come to the rooftop after dinner.

As per the plan, Shahnaz came to the rooftop around 10:00 at night. Even after spending a whole hour on Shahnaz's rooftop, when Rose didn't come to the rooftop, I also started feeling uneasy and understood that Rose didn't like the events of last night. Even after two hours had passed, when Rose didn't come to the rooftop, I went to the hostel rooftop with Shahnaz's help.

Where we had sat yesterday, I sat there again, and Shahnaz came to me. Some girls knew about my daily visits to the rooftop. Vandana had also seen me coming towards the rooftop. Shahnaz sat next to me there and kept talking about the same thing that I had been in love with Shahnaz for a long time. But my mind was focused on Rose and Rose's not coming upstairs.

I asked Shahnaz several times to call her upstairs, but she turned the talk by saying that Rose was not feeling well. Finally, I told Shahnaz - "Shahnaz, if you don't mind, can I sit here for the next 2 or 3 hours?" And then I told Shahnaz that I would definitely tell her the reason for my daily sitting on the rooftop tomorrow. After listening to me,

Shahnaz went downstairs.

For half an hour, I kept sitting on the rooftop alone like this, and then half an hour later, when Rose didn't come to the rooftop, I went to the girls' hostel rooftop with Shahnaz's help. Where we were sitting yesterday, I sat there again, and Shahnaz sat next to me.

When I kept asking her why she didn't come to the rooftop, she remained silent, without saying anything. When she didn't respond to my question for the next half an hour, I held her hand in mine and asked her why she didn't come to the rooftop. In response to my question, she said to me - Rose: "Can we claim our right on you or can you claim your right on us? Think and answer." Me: "Yes, of course, why not?" (I said with happiness in my heart) Rose: "Are you sure?"

Me: "Yes, why not! If we don't accept each other from the inside, we wouldn't be sitting here. Tell me, what do you want to say, understanding yourself?" I was happy inside because I knew that the three letters of love were about to come in front of me. And then I eagerly awaited the words that came out of those letters.

Rose asked me to close my eyes and told me that what she wanted to do, she couldn't do with my eyes open. Hearing all this, I also started feeling excited and closed my eyes. When I was feeling uncomfortable waiting with my eyes closed, suddenly I felt a slap on my cheek.

When I opened my eyes, there was no one around, just Rose sitting in front of me. Before I could ask her the reason for this, she started crying. When I wiped her tears and tried to make her silent, I felt that she had a high fever.

Here is the translation:

"I forgot to tell you one thing, I had a lot of trust in him, so I kept him quiet by giving him many promises, wanting to know the reason for the slap. Then he started all the things about Shahnaaz and me and then asked me: - "If we had a fever today, why did you call Shahnaaz to the roof and talk for hours? And then you came here to meet her again." Do you want to talk to Shahnaaz for us? Yes, I will try to talk to her only when I want to. No-no, we don't want that. Don't talk to her at all.

Now we have become such good friends, so don't talk to her at all. Okay, I won't talk to Shahnaaz.

I promise you. - I will do one more thing for you right now. "What?" I will tell you everything. And he reached out and put his hand on my head. He put his hand on my head.

Now you swear to me, for the next 5 minutes you will not do anything, you will just say it. Then he kept quiet and without saying anything, he kept looking at me. When I had made this promise to him, at that very moment, Shahnaaz came to the roof and sat down near us.

Shahnaaz was also continuously looking at us suspiciously, wondering what 'Saj' was going to say. I grabbed the wrist of his right hand with my right hand and as I stretched my left hand towards his head, holding it for a while like this, I came so close to him, his hair were tangled with mine, his eyes with mine, his face with mine, and his lips with mine.

After a few seconds like this, I moved back again. Shahnaaz looked surprised, looking at me with wide eyes, and to some extent even her mouth.

Even I smiled and said two such lines to her while leaving from there, which must have echoed in her ears even after I left. When I turned back in front of Shahnaaz, I moved back after turning my back and said -

Me: - Next time don't call me a friend, because we are not friends anymore. Love you - Love you and you Love me - Me-Me-Me- 'Everyday-Everyday-Everyday-Everyday'."

GHOST RIDERS IN LOVE STORY

"After sleeping for 2 to 3 hours in the morning, when we woke up and returned to the hostel after attending classes, we found out that a new student had been admitted to the 11th class, whose name was 'Abhishek'. Abhishek, like all other students' parents, provided him with food and drinks, extremely pleased with the culture of our room, they left for their own. When Abhishek returned to the room after leaving his parents, Kushagra and I welcomed him with some excellent toiletries and called him over.

So Abhishek said to me, 'I will complain to the warden about you, you are insulting me.' On hearing this, Kushagra sent a child from our room to call a child from the 12th class. While giving some toiletries to Abhishek in front of his parents, I asked Abhishek, 'Why did you go to see the 12th class student filling water even after hearing the

showers? Think a little and let out your hidden vanity and madness.'
Abhishek was also a little hesitant and took out some pictures from his pocket, putting them in the cupboard. Then began the task of assigning. When I was giving the task to Abhishek, he kept saying only one thing repeatedly, 'Brother, you give me any task, I will do it, but move my bed away from yours.' There were some reasons for Abhishek's saying this, which I will tell you about later in this chapter.

Since childhood, I had some strange incidents happening inside me, and even today they are. I will address them to you through some words. Upon saying this, there was a residence of some such situations, so I convinced everyone that nothing would be done because the pictures he brought and kept in the cupboard, I had seen some strange writings on them too.

I had just said this much when someone came to the gate for me, saying, 'Brother, SP Singh Sir has called you to the teacher's hostel roof.' As soon as he said this, all the big children in health were looking at me and I was looking at all of them with wide eyes.

And getting annoyed repeatedly, I was just asking that child, 'Did I get called for sure, and every time there was only one answer, yes brother, you got called.' I forgot to tell you their nature.

Perhaps I could not see any other teacher in it. Because the children of the heart were very innocent but where was the problem, this too will tell you. We students used to call these English teachers by the name of SP Singh, although his name was SP Singh, but we all children used to call him SP Singh 'Don'.

SP Singh Sir, no matter how much uproar was there in the class period, he used to leave all the children laughing and leave.

But after making a picture of that child's name. Actually, whenever he caught a complaint from a child, at that time a picture was made of that child's name, and that picture of SP Singh Don used to go to his hostel room and put it in a box. That big box was filled with pictures of children's names. When there was a complaint, the children were left laughing by making a picture and leaving, but whenever for any reason SP Singh Sir's mood was bad or mood was off, then he used to take out three or four pictures from the box.

And those three or four children with pictures were given the punishment of those complaints on the hostel roof, and that too for those mistakes which some child had made just 10 days ago and some child had made 6 months ago. On one side, the children had a lot of respect for the head because even after doing big mistakes, the children were left laughing.

So on the other hand, there was a lot of fear among the children because every child was called by the names of the pictures on the hostel roof, and all those children's service was done without any mercy for a full hour. Because the pictures were opened only when SP Singh Don's mood was off. According to this rule, to sleep in class and to treasure the treasures of excellent toiletries, I had made so many pictures, Singh Don used to say only one thing to me, 'son, if your picture comes out today, then no other picture will come out that day. That day, my entire hour will be spent for you.' And .... Ah ..... Today the number was mine. Upon hearing this news, all the friends started laughing and also became worried. They started making different assumptions.

How to avoid this trouble. And we all knew that there was no way to avoid it. At that time we were also devotees of Lord Mahadev. But, then what, taking the name of Lord Bholenath and with the firm waist of Kushagra, I started towards the teacher's hostel roof.

I already had a suspicion that any ill-minded friend could kill you for me SP Singh Don will not share the punishment. As a result, Kushagra also slipped away in the middle of the road. When I reached the teacher's hostel roof, I saw SP Singh standing alone on the entire roof. I smiled at him, in response to which he picked up a long stick kept nearby.

And he started towards me. Whenever any child came to this roof, the first thing was to lock the roof. Similarly, it happened to me too. SP Singh was coming towards me in full anger when suddenly a logic struck me. I thought son, today a strong hit is inevitable on you, why not try your logic and see, and I said to SP Singh Don - Me: - Sir, listen, see, the roof is locked, so I cannot escape anywhere. Why not you listen to my one thing first. After that, my mouth will not open for a full hour. Then your beating and my head. "

S.P. Singh: Speak quickly.

Me: Sir, just a while ago, some kids upstairs in the hostel ordered some items. The warden was out, so they ordered a total of 14-15 bottles. Maybe I know where all those bottles are stashed. If you want, I can get someone to search all the teachers.

I can tell you all the places where the bottles might be hidden, or if you prefer, I can quietly remove all the bottles tonight and give them to you, without anyone knowing. S.P. Singh, after hearing my long speech, seemed to have a little faith in me, thinking, "Maybe this boy will survive today."

Then S.P. Singh said, "How do you know that I drink?" I said, "Nobody told me, sir, but judging by your personality, it seems like you were in the army before. When you put on your black glasses and drive your car, you must know that all the kids call you 'Don'. Just by that personality, I guessed that when soldiers have a liking for something to drink, your personality must be even higher."

S.P. Singh: Chuckling, "Yes, even your madam 'Mrs.' asks me every day, and if you don't bring it tonight?"

"It doesn't mean anything, sir. If I couldn't bring it, you can summon me here, put a lock on the door right here on this roof."

S.P. Singh: "Okay, okay, fine. But listen, bring it at 11:00 at night, so no one sees. And if someone catches you, I'll beat you first and the most at night."

Singh looked around and said to me, "See, the boys

from the hostel are peeking from the windows to see your show, so go from here and sit in my room downstairs for an hour and read something.

And tell the kids that I requested the sir because it would be too humiliating here, so sir, lock yourself in the room and sleep." I went downstairs with S.P. Singh sir to his room. S.P. Singh sir introduced me to his wife (madam) and said that I'm a friend's son and if I bring something in the evening, she should keep it secret from anyone else. But when S.P. Singh was telling all these things to his wife, they were both winking at each other, and the madam at him.

Then I doubted that they both drink. Anyway, what did all this mean to me? Some snacks came in front with the salty biscuits, and I ate that snack and returned to the hostel. And one thing I forgot to tell you, S.P. Singh was Don (the most favored teacher of 45 days and the most favorite student of Shubhanshu, because Shubhanshu always got almost full marks in English. But this time was different because that night S.P. Singh was to be given a bottle, which Shubhanshu was sending.

I was going towards the roof of the Girls' Hostel, so there Shubhanshu was sending a bottle to S.P. Singh sir. When I reached the roof of the Girls'

Hostel, I told Rose about all these events (Abhishek and S.P.) happening during the day. First, he didn't believe me when he saw Shubhanshu returning from Teacher's Hostel.

We were both on the roof together. She was sitting and I was sitting with my head on the wall. She was stroking my hair with her hands. While lying like this, I asked her about Shahnaaz. So, she just said abruptly, "Rose: First of all, sorry for yesterday, whatever you did. Me: How many times do I have to apologize? Rose: Just once. Me: First, sorry for yesterday and this second sorry for now. Rose: For now! Why?

Me: You told me yourself, say sorry for yesterday. And saying sorry means saying sorry once for doing something wrong. And now there is a sorry due on you, which I want right now.

Rose: We're not. It doesn't happen like this. Me: Now shut up and don't speak. Let's go down to the sir. Bring it here a bit... a little more... that's it. This was the second time we did this. Then after that, I also forgot to count and maybe she did too. When both of us were continuing like this for quite a while, then suddenly Shahnaaz came to the roof, and I told Shahnaaz to come down with me and watch all this, so she went down saying, "If someone else had come upstairs, you two would have known."

Me: (To Rose) Does Shahnaaz get jealous? Well, she said it right. Rose: Oh, it's not like that, because some girls ask us by commenting, tell us what happened last night. You don't know these girls.

Me: Alright, leave that... bring your chair a bit closer. "You distribute favors according to your fate every day. You know that Sourav and Vandana haven't even touched each other properly yet. I've also forgotten properly." "Look, we're not.

You won't do anything wrong. Okay, sure. I won't do anything but I'll definitely see you touch. After that, for half an hour, both of us didn't know where we were. Maybe in those moments, I met a new Rose and about half or one hour later - "Sorry, we don't know what happened to us. Are we getting too close?"

"It seems like, you're still a bit less. By the way, let me tell you one thing: you were as dangerous as a snake like yesterday. Blushing, she placed her head on me and said, 'By the way, if I were smaller, would you hold me like your child? And how much better it would be if we lived together like this, me being Muslim and you Hindu. So what if our religions are not the same? How much closer we have come in just two or three days, isn't it? Maybe in our past life, we were husband and wife. We must have died early, that's why we are two years older and you're younger. Anyway, for marriage, you seem to have more feelings for us.

What does it mean for marriage? Alright... You were without feelings for the past two hours... - Oh no, crazy! You're completely crazy! We meant, in the past two hours, whatever was happening... (I said laughing) - Every day, we're not the same! You confuse us with your words. - I don't know, maybe. - What we were saying, you didn't even tell us.

We are Muslim and you are Hindu. How will our marriage happen, because our parents will beat us, they will kill us, they will not marry us to you. - Why worry? We'll elope. - Run away alone. We won't run away with you. You know? - Why? - Because we think that until your career is set up or our career is set up, running away means banging your head against the wall.

I was looking at her and she kept speaking continuously. Today, the Rose I was talking to wasn't the school Rose that everyone knew. I felt like a little child, being spoken to without understanding anything.

She kept speaking like that continuously and I just listened to her... Rose - You know, without a career setup, we face a lot of difficulties.

Our aunt's daughter also eloped once. Those who run away, even the police chase them, they become criminals, and when they get money, they die hungry. - (I said laughing at her childish talk) Alright... die hungry... Rose - Yes... Haven't you seen what's written in newspapers and on news channels, how many people died of hunger? They are the ones who run away from home. Like that, one day our names will also come, that people died of hunger.

Listening to her childish talks, I also smiled amusedly. Up to here, I managed to control myself. But from here onwards, I couldn't stop myself, and I kept laughing continuously. And she kept looking at me like a child. After a minute, I controlled my laughter and asked - Where are you from, friend?

Are you the same Rose who was the topper in 11th Biology and who doesn't let any guy get close, and if you're the same Rose, then who's this 2-year-old child? I meet you every night... - I don't know, friend, earlier when we didn't talk much to you, it was fine. But in 2 or 3 days, it feels like there's no one closer to us than you.

When we used to fight, sometimes we felt like talking to you, but we stopped ourselves. Alright! Now that the running away plan has failed, what about our future? - You're crazy... (cutting her off) You're crazy! (cutting her off) You're crazy! - Hey crazy, let me finish. In Hinduism, Radha-Krishna is considered the epitome. Do you know why? Because it's a symbol of true love, and our love is also true, right?

Although Krishna had other marriages, but even today, without marriage, he and Radha are still together. We'll also live like that. (she said smiling) I couldn't understand how to respond to her words. I also listened to her childish talks with amusement.

Then suddenly Rose said something that made me restless. Rose, looking troubled, said - Let me tell you one thing, after you leave, when we're sleeping, we keep getting a thought in our mind repeatedly, and we feel like we'll get angry with you for some reason for many years and we'll know that you're troubled without us, but still, we'll stay angry and won't meet you for many years."

Here is the English translation of the provided Hindi paragraph:

"Mamu: Alright, we need an excuse to fight (said with a smile). Rose: No, dude, that's not it. The problem is that we know we won't be able to stay angry with you for more than a day or two.

Then ultimately, what mistake will you make that we'll stay angry for many years? Mamu: Okay, leave it, it must just feel that way.

Just think less negatively. Rose: I know, just now we were feeling the same way. Mamu: Don't worry, crazy, even if you get angry, I'll come to you after a few days and persuade you. Just then, the hostel boys started shouting loudly. I looked around and saw the noise was coming from the room.

I went to the bathroom area and saw Kushagra drinking quietly with Dada. Hearing the noise, Kushagra also stood up, and from below, he shouted at me, 'Hey, bro, get out of here quickly, this trouble is from our own room. Abhishek has created some drama, before we reach the teacher's room, we have to go there.

' Hearing all this, I immediately went downstairs to leave, and I was thinking to myself that in trying to avoid one problem, I sent Rs 5000 worth of alcohol to ASP Singh and here, this trouble again. It was clear to me that both of them were going to fight that night.

Quickly, we both reached our room in the hostel. The scene in the room was like this. All the kids were standing on their beds. Some had shoes in their hands, some had slippers. Both PTIs were standing separately in corners. Those who had reached there before us. As soon as we reached our room, everyone's attention was on us, and my attention was on Abhishek, who was standing in the middle of the room - his hair was disheveled and his shirt was torn. Both PTIs were staring at me and Kushagra as if once Abhishek's matter was settled, they were going to take their anger out on us.

That was the only quality in me that Kushagra was also crazy about, that whenever he saw me, he felt like all the ways to escape were blocked, so I made things worse, even in the hope that perhaps now... That's it, then. I, continuing on this path, to let out all my frustration, picked up a shoe lying nearby and showered Abhishek with it.

Upon doing this, Kushagra and a few other boys also pounced on him. A few moments later, both PTIs came forward and separated us, and I just kept saying to the PTI head, 'Sir, just leave me for a while. Today, I'm exorcising this ghost. You know, sir, just 10 minutes ago, Kushagra and I understood this, that we're becoming angels in just 10 minutes.

This is not a case of back and forth, sir, this scoundrel is making a fool of himself.' Both PTIs instructed everyone to sleep and left, saying if this matter comes up again tomorrow, then from the day after tomorrow, we both will sleep like this again.

All the lights in our room were turned off, and everyone went to sleep. I too was sleeping next to that Abhishek Samrat (Abhishek's full name).

Two things were bothering me a lot. First, that I knew there was some affair going on with Abhishek Samrat, but was it just common, or something else?

And the second thing was troubling me that I

knew what happened today would happen with Abhishek Samrat tomorrow as well.

And if that happened, then both PTIs would sleep with us in this room, so should we stop meeting Rose, or was I secretly thinking about the solution to this Samrat's ghost's affair..."

SOME LAST WISHES

As soon as I woke up in the morning, I had only one thought in my mind, how to cure this obsession of Abhishek Samrat. Throughout the day, both Kushagra and I kept thinking about it, but nothing seemed to make sense.

As I told you, we all give some good reason or the other to catch wrong habits, which is very wrong for us. Just like Kushagra and I were, devotees of Lord Baba Bholenath. It was 7:00 in the evening, and we had finished eating and were going towards the hostel when suddenly Shahnaz came to me and said, "Tell me something about Rose that you have never told me before."

I replied, 'Alright,' and watched her angrily as she walked to her hostel. Kushagra and I went to the roof of our boys' hostel and started thinking about the cure for Abhishek Samrat's ghostly obsession.

And when no solution came to mind, I lay down on the roof and started making fun of most of the boys in the hostel, so Kushagra replied to my words, "Friend, 80% of the boys in this hostel are so foolish that they don't even know that so much dirty work is done in the hostel every day, and in the remaining 20%, most of them are such that they don't even benefit from studying. How amazing is hostel life, isn't it?"

Saying all this, Kushagra flicked his cigarette into the air and said, "Hey, Baba Bholenath, now you tell me the cure for this Abhishek's ghostly obsession."

Kushagra said this and I looked at the cigarette in my hand and asked Kushagra to fill it, and Kushagra said, "Son, now tighten the next 5-6 cigarettes a bit more and then ..." After that, I called Abhishek Samrat by shouting at a boy. Now there were three people on the roof: me, Kushagra, and Abhishek Samrat.

The gate of the roof was closed from the roof side and then we made Abhishek sit next to us on the roof and said, "Friend, sorry for last night. The atmosphere was such that we had to do it.

Now that you are a friend, forgive me." Abhishek replied, "No friend, it's okay. Kushagra-No, no friend, you didn't forgive, don't lie. You are still upset about the matter. Right? Abhishek - No brother, it's not like that. I have been in this situation for many years.

Many medicines were also tried, but many old men and others did not benefit much. Kushagra - (said to me) You tell him your way of fixing it, correcting it. (Said to Abhishek) Take this cigarette and drink it quickly, because there is medicine inside. Abhishek - (said to me) No brother, I don't drink all this. You are misunderstanding me.

Me - (to Abhishek) Put it in your mouth quietly, or else we will pick you up together from the roof and drop you downstairs, and tell everyone that you got dizzy due to Abhishek's ghostly obsession. Abhishek - (arguing with both of us) You guys don't know me and you don't know the standards of my family either.

I will fix you both in a way that you will remember it for a lifetime. Kushagra - (to Abhishek) This fool is joking. He got up. Abhishek - (said to both of us) Look, brothers, if you force me like this, but if you ask me lovingly in the name of friendship, I will definitely drink it. Kushagra - (to Abhishek) What were you doing in the police station for so long?

After that, I gave Abhishek Samrat a little training, and then the mahfil started. One by one, Abhishek Samrat smoked a 'full cigarette', and as soon as we thought its effect was over, even after the seventh, we gave him more and more cigarettes and then, took him down to his bed in the room and laid him there.

And from all the boys, I said, if anyone asks about Abhishek Samrat, tell them that medicine came from his house today and he is sleeping after taking it.

Here's the translation of the provided text from Hindi to English:

My planning regarding Abhishek Samrat was so simple that I just had to get him intoxicated to such an extent that even if some ghost or deity came to lift him, he wouldn't be able to get up from the bed for 6-7 hours.

After that, I also informed all the kids in the room that if any teacher comes at night, they should stand by the window (towards the girls' hostel) and shout loudly, "Sir, don't wake him up, or else a ghost will come."

I had arranged this window thing for myself and

Kushagra so that as soon as any teacher came to our room at night, we could quickly retreat.

After that, Kushagra went to Dadda's place, and I stayed near Rose. I sat near Rose for about 3 to 4 hours, and she kept crying continuously for those 4 hours. Even after repeatedly asking her, she didn't say anything. When I tried to get close to her, she kept crying incessantly.

The atmosphere had become such that seeing her crying so much, I also started crying with her. It was really strange that a guy like me, who never cried for himself, was crying because of a girl's tears. We cried until 4:00 in the morning, and when she didn't stop, I said to her, "Okay, if you're crying because of me, then fine, I'll leave tomorrow." (She said to me) "Yes, please leave, and if you ever talk to Shahnaaz in life, don't look at me again. And if you don't talk, then come a little earlier tomorrow, we have something to do."

I was just looking towards her with empathy, wondering why she had been crying all night, with whom I had spoken to Shahnaaz. After apologizing to her and admitting my mistake, I walked her down to the gate. This was the first time I was apologizing to someone.

I didn't know what I was becoming or rather what she was making me become. This was the fifth night of our relationship. After apologizing, we both came down to the gate, then wished each other good night and then I went to my room and she went to hers.

I still remember that day, it was July 26th, a Monday. After doing the morning prayers, I went to class. After the lunch break, I and Kushagra were roaming outside after eating. Suddenly, a boy wearing the school uniform comes in front of me and starts giving me abuses.

Before I could understand anything, Kushagra, laughing, leaves me there and goes away, and when that boy abused me and left, Kushagra came back to me and started asking, "Hey, why are you laughing while getting abused by that guy, and why did your face turn red when he was abusing you?" I replied, "Because I recognized this boy's face from before.

Let's find out the matter, what it is." We followed that boy and saw Rose and Shahnaaz sitting with her parents and brother in an empty classroom. I had just reached the room when Rose's brother said to his father, "Dad, this is the 'Kaafir'." Ignoring her brother's words, I greeted her parents with folded hands.

As a result, I didn't get a response to the greeting, but her father stared at me and said, "Son, Saj has told me that you are his good friend, so I'm explaining to you to just focus on studies and leave all this useless friendship, etc." I chuckled and said, "Uncle, you have explained to me quite late again, I had already understood it before you." Internally, while looking at Rose, I was saying to myself, "What a creature you are, sometimes you seem like a sensible girl of this world, and sometimes like the mind of a 1-year-old child."

Just then, Kushagra's voice came from behind the class gate, saying, "Come on, he will either bring the passport or the whole purse with him."

Even after coming back from the class, I greeted Rose's parents and left. There was still no response from them. Coming outside, I said to Kushagra, "There won't be any marriage, friend. Just get me to sign the papers today itself.

Now, it seems I'll have to run away with her. By the way, let me tell you, sometimes there's a twist of fate even for... is ther any age group problems exist before run up or not ?

The translation of the provided text to English is as follows:

"Kushagra, getting married to Girls seems like a distant dream. Your family won't even allow you to enter the house, and I have no idea when that might happen, buddy. You must know him from his neighborhood, right?"

Kushagra: "Yes, I'm certainly from his neighborhood, but in our family..."

After that, I and Kushagra returned to our hostel. It was evening, and our room's windows were all open. In the room, Kushagra saw a small child smoking a cigarette, which boosted the child's enthusiasm.

At that moment, my attention fell on the hostel's window, from which I used to see the child with a cigarette in his mouth every day. Then, I went to the child and slapped him hard twice. The biggest surprise was what I saw in front of me. Even after slapping him twice, the child was staring at me with eyes wide open, just like Kushagra. Kushagra, with astonishment in his eyes, said, "Has a teacher come? Has someone come to teach?" I replied, "No, buddy, this is all wrong. Haven't you seen? He's just a child."

Kushagra: "Oh, gods of the righteous, tell me, was this child's first cigarette given to him, and was he taught to smoke and eat it upside down?"

Then, we heard a voice from the hostel's window: "show"

Hearing the voice of the word 'showoff', Kushagra said to me, "By God, I didn't know she was watching all this every day."

After that, I explained a lot of helping verbs to Kushagra, and then a while later, both of us looked at the child on whom I had slapped. He was still sitting on his bed, staring at me with wide eyes and holding a cigarette, asking me, "Brother, is this for smoking or not?"

Hearing his words, Kushagra and I burst into laughter. And then I said to him again, "No, son, you should never smoke again. Just now I saw that your sister-in-law has gone back, stopping you. Look, she's still standing at the back window." I turned around to look back, and she was laughing while waving. I said, "This isn't show-off, Rose knows it," and blushed as I closed the window. It was time for dinner. After dinner, Rose came to me for a moment or two and said, "You enjoy so much, bring all this stuff with you a little every night, but don't bring it all at once."

I was deeply concerned about what was going to happen today and then after that. And then, I and Kushagra mesmerized Rohit, then Kushagra went to Dada. I asked with a worried expression, "Why did you order so much stuff (taking out bottles from the pocket and showing)? Rose said, "You will leave all these bad habits from today."

I said, "Drinking all this is not a bad habit because maybe you don't know that Lord Bholenath is an ascetic, and they also drink bhang. Everything is beyond your system, so leave all this."

Kushagra: "Okay, sir! We're out of your system. You're very clever."

Here's the translation of the provided text:

"We know this much, whenever you tread on the footsteps of God, walk with full conviction. Lord Shiva does a lot more, you do all of that too.

Stop wearing artificial things, leave aside all these clothes. They are ascetic, so you become ascetic too, and don't hold any attachment for anyone. If their habits are taking over you, then take them all. You know, we've heard that once when his wife, Devi Sati, got immersed in the yajna, they were about to end the whole world, if something like that happens with you, will you also end the world?

You know, I've heard that Lord Bholenath drinks bhang, that's why I also drink. You don't have any desire to become a god. Just Goddess, I give up.

I understood, if I don't stop drinking all this and if by any chance something happens to you, then this world will be destroyed (I joked). - So keep your hand on my head and swear, that you'll leave all these bad habits from today onwards, and if you don't leave these habits today, I swear that you'll see my dead face.

Putting a hand on the head every day and swearing, and then saying every day - today I won't do this anymore, but today, you'll also do a little with me, and then after that, she laughed and agreed.

They both teased each other a little and smoked a little. He touched the drink only with his tongue, and also the smoke, just to keep me company. We had already agreed on the sixth night a day earlier. I slowly approached her and kept reducing the physical distance between us. At first, she hesitated a bit but after a while, she was so quiet as if she agreed with my sentiment.

This sixth night of our relationship, was such a first night when we both slowly, slowly crossed some boundaries, lost in an intoxication...

We both, lost in intoxication, lost in a trance-like state, got lost in such a way... we didn't even realize when we went astray. Even the moon was a witness to that crazy night. When we ourselves, in our own intoxication, got lost in each other.

After an hour, both of us, looking at each other again, started apologizing for whatever happened. For a while, both of us sat quietly, and then after a while, seeing each other embarrassed, we laughed.

It was also the first time with her, that day she also told me about a boy named 'Sumit' who came into her life and also about getting engaged with 'Sumit'.

I again put my hand on her head and she said - "I swear, in my life, no girl will come other than you"| Everyday - If we couldn't get married, then

Me - I'll stand on my feet and take you with me| Everyday - And if we don't go together, then don't misunderstand us| We will always stay with each other like Radha-Krishna| Me - If you leave me for some reason later and leave me, then.

Everyday - We won't do that for sure. And yes, listen, tomorrow evening, along with some teachers, we're all going for the 'Govardhan Puja' and 'Janmabhoomi', and in that tour, we'll go with you. And going with you, we'll ask for blessings from all the gods. And you tell me one crazy thing, when Radha-Krishna, who are true to love, have never separated till today, then how will we? We won't. But don't betray me either.

Just love me. Me - And if you betray me? Then? Everyday - We're swearing by putting our hands on your head that until your face, your voice, your name, any part of you, and our love will be remembered, until then no other boy will be there in our life, leaving our husband. A long, long oath has been taken.

I couldn't say it directly, I'll come. - We don't know, we're not. We ate whatever came to our minds, there's only one thing in both oaths. After that, while descending, we both made our way to our rooms in our own way, with our own estimates of each other's nights on the stairs. Another day passed, and in the evening, going to the temple, all the children of the tour went with us.

As per the plan, as we had promised each other one night before, every day, fulfilling all promises, she went ahead.

She stood in front of the Radha-Krishna temple, and stood next to me, promising her truthfulness, and went with our eternal love. That day, holding the hand of all the teachers, Krishna promised in the temple that he would never betray me, and also reiterated those promises himself.

Near the temple, we found a place where names were being written on the body with a machine. She wrote my name on my hand with her own hands, the name she used to call me by. When she was writing my name with the machine on my hand, there was a lot of pain, so she made a letter 'A' under the sole of my foot.

When we were returning to the hostel late at night, she, speaking loudly in front of the madam and sir, said to me in a loud voice, "Sir, whatever we have asked for here, will be fulfilled, we will come here every year."

But she was wrong, she was wrong about everything she said. Because after that day, neither did she ever come there, nor did she ever think of coming there."

A LOVE KING

"When my eyes opened on the second day, like every morning, I found a cigarette hidden in the room. It reminded me of my daily struggle. Determined, I extinguished the cigarette and headed out for a run.

I had been trying hard to quit this bad habit for several days. There was another boy named Ram Bharat who had been following me and Kushagra for a long time. He wanted us to tell him some ways to impress a girl named Raashi from our class 10th.

We had been suggesting him some ways to impress girls, which he diligently followed. Eventually, he became friends with Raashi. Ram Bharat was completely rustic, but his biggest enemy was his overweight. To befriend Raashi, he did exactly as we advised.

During lunchtime, Ram Bharat came to us and asked, 'Brother, Raashi is alone in the girls' hostel right now, and all the other girls have gone downstairs to the hostel mess for lunch. If you permit, I can go up there now.' We refused and went to have lunch. Another amusing thing was that Ram Bharat used to tell Raashi that his friendship with her was because of us. Kushagra and I sat in the mess for lunch.

After about 3 minutes, I suddenly glanced around the mess, and I saw that Ram Bharat was not there. I immediately left my food and rushed outside the mess, and Kushagra also quickly followed. We had only reached the gate of the girls' hostel when Ram Bharat came running from inside the hostel and, with folded hands, said, 'I've been telling you for so many days to teach me something, but you never did.'

'Hey...(helping verb), did I teach you to do this? I told you not to go upstairs...' That's all I had said when Ram Bharat cut me off and ran shouting towards the boys' hostel – 'Save yourself today, no matter what, I will follow you for the rest of my life, wherever you go.' Kushagra – (to me) Brother, something big is about to happen. Because yesterday evening, he was telling me that he had told Raashi that he would try something new with her, our love. But I didn't tell him how to kiss her.

Now quickly, let's find out some more girls from the hostel mess to make sure everything is fine. Kushagra sent 2-3 girls upstairs to Raashi. About 3 minutes later, all the girls came down with Raashi and started heading towards the office. Raashi's cheeks were bleeding a lot, indicating that someone had slapped her hard on the face.
Seeing the blood on Raashi's cheeks and tears in her eyes, and she continuously staring at me, it was clear that someone had hit her on the face.

She kept staring at me as if I was responsible for everything. Then, while leaving with Raashi, she kept saying, 'You did all this, right?' I looked angrily at Kushagra and started searching for Ram Bharat in the hostel.

I took a shoe in my hand – ahead, and Kushagra followed me from behind to stop me. After struggling for a while, Ram Bharat was found. He was locked in a toilet, whose door he had locked from the inside.

After giving him several scoldings, I became quiet when he said to me, 'Brother, if you hadn't saved me today, I would have gone upstairs and jumped from the roof.' My anger subsided, and then both Kushagra and I lovingly escorted him out and took him to our room, explaining to him along the way.

Actually, Raashi got trapped in Ram Bharat's

scheme too quickly because Ram Bharat was very handsome and had a sweet way of speaking. Raashi didn't know that the true nature of every boy is not seen in front of his parents or girls.

If boys ever show their true nature, it is only in front of their friends, which is also true. I took Ram Bharat to my room, on one hand, I was consoling him, nothing wrong will happen, I am with you, and on the other hand, I was trying to control myself, so that I don't consume any intoxicants. But despite all my efforts, I couldn't stop myself for long, and when Kushagra and I went towards the roof to treat Abhishek Samrat's ghost, I also couldn't stop myself from doing all this, which I had been swearing off every day.

From one perspective, we were doing wrong with Abhishek Samrat, as if we were getting him intoxicated as soon as it got dark. Abhishek Samrat seemed happy because now no spirit or ghost in the world had the power to break our bond and could scare Abhishek Samrat.

Our intention was not to treat any ghost. All these gimmicks were done by me to meet daily. Meanwhile, I, Kushagra, and Abhishek Samrat were lost in our intoxication, where I was thinking inside out about how this intoxication is the last today, and on the other hand, Rose saw me doing all this from the roof of the hostel.

Around 11:00, I reached near Rose , who was quite angry. Despite apologizing many times by me, she remained silent, and when I was asked to give some oaths, she said angrily to me – 'What, did you accept my oaths? I tried my best. But you won't understand because you don't know how such habits are left.

I'm not saying you're wrong, but maybe there are some things that you can't understand. Because you won't get some things.'"

"If you were doing all this, you would definitely understand," Rose said, "We don't think we need to understand anything here, but you definitely need to explain some things. Right?"

"One thing always remember, my dear," Rose continued, "If you ever want to leave anything in life, it happens in a second. Things don't leave gradually. Gradually leaving means you haven't fully agreed to leave yet. And these things apply to everything in the world. I told you about Sumit; you know he used to be very flattering to me but there was something else behind my back.

Yes, all boys are like that, not just Sumit. Every day we don't think you're like that, but we want to explain to you that we left him in a moment forever. Even though he stayed in our minds for months, we left him means we really left him. But don't you think Sumit should be given another chance?

Opportunities have certain limits. Today, our relationship with you, if you make a mistake in this relationship, we should give you a chance. Because we believe that before forming any close relationship, it should be thoroughly examined, and if it is wrong in the examination, then that relationship should be ended in the first place.

If a relationship has become close to you, then you should give it a chance, because the other person will not wrong you forever. Someday he will realize how wrong he is doing with a good person. You know, Anikesh, if we wrong you, no one can stop us, not even you. We can even say wrong things and catch you.

But as long as you love us in your heart, if we do something wrong, the guilt inside us will eat us up because we are doing wrong with the person who is our world. And if there is no guilt inside, then?

When someone goes against the soul, then it is

determined by God or the Almighty. Where do all these things come from within you?" "I don't know, but sometimes I really want to teach you everything, because sometimes I feel like I'm getting all this knowledge back from you if we ever make a mistake.

I have never forgotten all these things told by you, and I have seen all this in every other person's relationship. In a young age, she said such things to me that perhaps no one else could say wrong in life. Even today, I wait, hoping I could understand her and her words again.

After that, when I asked her about Raashi, she told me that Raashi had four marks on her cheek and yesterday Ram Bharat had called Raashi's parents. 'Ram Bharat's name might also be cut off,'

Rose said. 'No, it won't happen. Somehow or the other, I saved Ram Bharat yesterday. - Why would you save Ram Bharat? Listen to me carefully, you will never support a wrong person.

And that's why not even Ram Bharat tomorrow. Do you enjoy doing something wrong to someone? And yes, what were you saying? Did I make him do all this?" "Hey, we're just saying what's the need for you to teach anyone anything.

Those who teach and help like this are always for everyone. So don't think you're the only one, okay? If you could, you'd change me completely." "We're not changing, just telling you some good things," Rose said. "For a long time, I lay in his lap, and we kept talking like this.

While talking, Rose told me about a function at Rose's house tomorrow. After saying this much, she became a little sad and quiet when I asked the whole thing, she said - "Nothing, friend, there is a function at home tomorrow.

Two days ago when the family came, they were going to take me along for this function. I didn't go because of you, and I made an excuse for a class test because I wanted to stay with you.

We're telling the truth that something like this is happening with us for the first time, that someone feels dearer to us than our family and our heart is making us not to go. Okay, who is that person? Even our wedding?"

"Everyday - No way. The day we discussed marriage at home, from that day onwards, they will become our enemies. We have other dreams too that we want to fulfill.

Me - Yes, the computer teacher told you, you want to become a computer security expert, and you are quite knowledgeable. Everyday - 'Yes, I am the boss.' Okay, today I'll tell you another dream, which we will fight with our family to fulfill.

Me - What? (Asked in surprise) - We want to become a very big Bollywood actress. We know it's quite difficult, but for some reason, we feel that with your help, it might become easier. Will you help us? Always - I will always do. But don't forget our deal, don't forget why. Nowadays, you can't tell, there are so many beautiful boys or girls in this world. - Crazy, you are not more beautiful than us. - Let's see. - Okay, now it's time, the day is about to end.

I went a little closer to you. Even though you remained silent for 5 or 10 minutes, but when that day also started crossing some limits, I suddenly stopped you and said - No, not today, please.

Why? - We are not ready. When we say, just accept it. Then when? - On returning. When you return, you won't refuse then, will you?

I swear you will see my dead face if you refuse. - We don't say that. We are not refusing. Suddenly, I started walking towards the hostel, and you said, stop. I stopped. You came close to me, and bending down, you touched your head with both your feet, and said - Whenever we go away from you, we will touch your feet like this. And if we come from somewhere else, we will come and touch your feet.

And you know, we wished in Radha Krishna's temple, in Krishna Janmabhoomi, that until we do this, Lord Krishna will always keep us together, and you always say that it's very true - hail Bihari Lal! Seeing your childish antics and unwavering faith in Radha Krishna, tears welled up in my eyes.

I cried, pulled you down again next to me, held your feet, made you barefoot again, and then I cried with my eyes, kissed your feet on the same spot where I wrote 'A'. I don't know why tears in my eyes were not stopping, and while kissing your feet, I said - Whenever you come, I will welcome you like this every time.

Again you came down to leave me like every day, and your last words that day were - "Listen, come back soon." I don't know why that day, I didn't sleep even in the hostel, and again went to class with Chahar. As I told you, according to my daily routine, I give my time to my work and my parents' goals.

According to that goal, after finishing school, I used to come straight to class and remember all the subjects taught that day.

After an hour of break, when I was sitting in class studying, suddenly a boy came running into the class and said to me - "Come on, Kushagra is calling you." That boy said this and left. But I didn't change my ways, and again I kept studying continuously, because during my study time, I don't give it anywhere else.

That's why even after studying for 2 hours, I was still at the top of the class. After the break, while studying in class, Ajay was also studying sitting next to me. Ajay: This Kushagra is also strange, brother. He knows you won't go anywhere at this time, strange friend, right? - The more true friends there are, brother, the more this joke is common. (laughs). - By the way, there are many chachers in the hostel nowadays, yours.

Become big LOVE, then continue to love. - (Laughing) Sure, take anyone's oath, I didn't give Ram Bharat this advice. - Are you distributing knowledge to others or is there any hidden motive for yourself too? - Earlier I thought of it as a deal, but then I fell in love. Now I feel like becoming the LOVE KING for that QUEEN. There are very big dreams of his, so why not turn this life into those dreams now? - Oye hoye my lover, now you're going to become LOVE KING.

:- (Smiling) Yeah, buddy... I'll have to become one. Because only he can fulfill such big dreams. Ajay puts his pencil down and hits my shoulder with his shoulder. -

:- (Smiling) What's his name, tell us too. On Ajay's

question, I smile and my gaze falls on Kushagra standing at the gate. Kushagra wanted to say something but couldn't. Tears welled up in his eyes, and he was just looking at me.

Then 2-3 girls came behind Kushagra and one of the girls said to me - "Rose is no more, she's not here anymore...."

Kushagra completed her sentence with tears in his eyes. "She's no longer here, friend, she's no longer in this world. I've confirmed it by calling multiple times." My whole mind was numb; I couldn't understand what I was hearing.

After a few moments, I had also forgotten whether someone was standing around me or not. My eyes remained wide open; tears kept flowing incessantly, my mouth was agape.

People around me were talking, but I couldn't hear anything. Tears continued to flow from my eyes, my heart stopped, and I was just lost in her memories. Now there was nothing left far and wide.

If anything remained, it was just a desperate desire, a longing, to meet her again, to have her again.

ITS JUST A BEGINNING

For 4 hours, I sat there in the same class, lost in thoughts. Now, if there was anything, it was just the familiar feeling of her hands in mine that I always felt with her.

I remembered that moment when after my last words, she held my hand tightly. I felt like my world was ending, but for some reason, her hand was still in mine. The realization of her presence with me was comforting. My mind and body were feeling increasing discomfort every moment, unable to control even though I wanted to, and now, even that control seemed elusive.

The day and night passed in tears. But from the next day, I was consumed in silence. The madness of being lost in solitude took over me. I cried anywhere and everywhere like a madman.

Just seeing Shahnaaz made me cry, I cried while eating, and often, I cried just looking towards

the washroom in school where we had our first meeting and altercation. When nothing could be understood about how to live or survive, I was overcome with madness, and leaving the hostel became necessary to avoid becoming crazy.
The biggest concern sending me back home was Kushagra.

He was not wrong in his place because some actions had escalated to such an extent, like going to the terrace of the girls' hostel at night alone and getting the feeling that she was with me there, going overboard with intoxication, and feeling that some teachers knew about my intoxication and getting lost in my own intoxication.

Here, Kushagra also took care of me as a good friend so that my indulgence in intoxication wouldn't become the cause of our infamy.

So, to be lost in solitude, the crutch of dry intoxication was used. And in my solitude, lost, I was increasingly consumed by the memories of my first love. Do you know what was that first love?

No, no, not Rose... In every corner of my soul and body, just one name resided, Mahadev $$$$... my innocent Lord. Oh! I forgot to tell you my name.

I'm Nag Thenua, and this was my and Rose's love

story, which, like yours, was being felt by me too.

Yes, this story has ended now, but this was just the beginning.

The real story was still left because someone knew that after a few years, she would return with new names and new forms.

Was someone returning with a new name after a few years?

Would Nag Thenua recognize Rose in her new face?

After Rose's departure, what would happen to Nag Thenua?

Would he become very bad after leaving Rose's memories?

Would the girls now become a toy to play for him? Would 'Nag' become a social outcast leaving all bad habits?

Whose purpose of living would now be to fulfill

Rose's dreams, will he become the world's greatest computer hacker?

Or will he go to Bollywood's dark alleys, where nothing is found except disappointments?

And how would be his first meeting with Rose now, would there be a challenge this time due to the generation gap?

TO BE CONTINUED.........

SHE IS BACK– This Time With A Hate Story PART -2 - THEME

" Forgetting, they saw every scene of their love, became lean, and entered Lord Bholenath. They again forgot them, some new game started in the park, and in this game, new names and new forms were given, and the new beginning also started. "

LIFE OF THORNS– A Journey Towards Bollywood PART - 3 - THEME

" Seeing reality, words became a support, I kept saying something, then someone brought such a love, which I had come to endure. His intention was his own, to reach his destiny to the stars, I stayed among the stars with you. "